HER WILDE M_____

Wilde, Nevada 4

Chloe Lang

MENAGE EVERLASTING

Siren Publishing, Inc.
www.SirenPublishing.com

A SIREN PUBLISHING BOOK
IMPRINT: Ménage Everlasting

HER WILDE MARINES
Copyright © 2014 by Chloe Lang

ISBN: 978-1-62741-512-5

First Printing: July 2014

Cover design by Les Byerley
All art and logo copyright © 2014 by Siren Publishing, Inc.

Printed in the U.S.A.

PUBLISHER
Siren Publishing, Inc.
www.SirenPublishing.com

DEDICATION

Chloe Vale works so hard on all my books. Her input is invaluable. She's the queen of grammar and a dear friend whose encouragement always helps me make the stories of Wilde and Destiny richer.

This one is for you, sweetie.

HER WILDE MARINES

Wilde, Nevada 4

CHLOE LANG
Copyright © 2014

Chapter One

"Emma, we're coming for you."

Emma Grant sat up in her bed, jolted awake by the voices of her dead sisters. Sweat beaded on her forehead, and her heart raced. The nightmare seemed so real. From the darkness of her dream her sisters Samantha and Lily had called to her again and again.

Trembling from the aftermath, she pulled her sheet up to her chin. *This is only a dream. This is only a dream. This is only a dream.*

Emma repeated the mantra over and over that she'd created soon after her mother and Lily's funeral in Wilde. That's when the nightmares had begun. Why couldn't she stop dreaming about her troubled, homicidal, mentally ill sisters? She'd tried sleeping pills but that had only made things worse.

Emma knew sleep had escaped her for the rest of the night, so she leaned over and clicked on her lamp. She flung off the blanket and grabbed her robe. A cup of hot tea might calm her nerves.

She stood and heard a creaking noise that made her freeze in position.

What is it? You're letting your imagination get the better of you, Em.

"Emma. Emma. Emma."

Her heart thudded like a jackhammer in her chest.

This wasn't a dream. She was actually hearing Lily's voice.

No. This can't be happening to me, too.

"We're coming for you, Em. Be ready." Samantha's voice sounded faint but she could hear every syllable.

Shaking, she leaned back on her bed and brought her hands to her face. She remained there for what seemed like several minutes.

Finally Emma knew she had to face her demons and fears. She must go to Wilde, her hometown and the place where her sisters had committed all the horrors.

She went to check on her children. Both Andrea and Autumn were sound asleep, completely unaware of what she'd been suffering and of the voices she'd also been hearing. A good thing. Andrea was thirteen and Autumn twelve. Too young to think their mother was going crazy.

There's no sense kidding myself any longer. I have what Sam, Lil, and our dad had.

She closed her girls' door quietly and headed into the kitchen. A cup of tea might not cure mental illness, but she thought it might help to clear her head for the moment. She needed a moment. Several, actually, but she would settle for just one.

She started the kettle and leaned back against the counter to wait for the water to get hot.

As soon as the sun came up, she would call her grandparents and tell them her plans. She'd been keeping up appearances for them and the girls. Hell, for everyone.

Don't let them see you crack up, Em, or they'll shove you in a loony bin.

* * * *

"This is Hammer. Target is in view, Eagle. Permission to engage. Copy." Marine Corps Major Bane Taylor's team of seven was in position.

"Roger that, Hammer. Hold for confirmation."

Three thousand miles away in Libya, a similar mission was being conducted by Bane's identical twin brother, Adam, the same rank as he. Only their mother and dads could tell them apart. They'd done everything together and could even finish each other's sentences. Of course, he and Adam were different in some ways. Adam was the more fun loving of them, whereas he was the flip side, the more serious twin.

Both classified operations, the one here in Somalia and the one in Libya, were critical in the war on terror. Intel had identified key Al-Qaeda operatives, which HQ wanted dead or alive.

One last mission, then Adam and I will go home.

He and his brother had seen a ton of action during their tours. They'd been lucky, having never been wounded. But luck eventually ran out for everyone. They'd lost so many brothers in arms on the battlefields around the world. During their last leave, they'd agreed to volunteer for the latest RIF the military was offering. Their commanding officer had tried to convince them to stay in, but they knew it was time to get out. They were highly decorated, but they would never be able to speak of their secret missions.

It was time to return home to Wilde, which was dealing with a war of its own. The FBI, to combat the drug cartel targeting Wilde and the surrounding areas, had recruited him and Adam. The kingpin of the criminal organization, Ricardo Delgado, had vanished after his cousin was killed in Wilde. Austin and Sheriff Champion were working together to bring down the bastard.

"Permission granted to engage the target, Hammer. God be with you."

* * * *

Adam Taylor leaned back in his seat on the transport plane. His last mission had been a complete success. No casualties. The two Al-

Qaeda operatives were already out of the country and in the hands of the US at a secret location. A great ending to a wonderful military career. He was anxious to move on.

Bane's mission had been successful, too. His three high-level targets had been taken alive. Unfortunately, one of his twin's men had been shot. Even though the soldier would survive, Bane, being Bane, would replay the event in his mind over and over looking for any crack or flaw in the plan. Adam knew there would be none. The mission was only as good as the intelligence provided. The Somalia information had some gaps, like an inaccurate count of the number of Al-Qaeda in the house Bane's team raided. It was a miracle that there hadn't been more wounded or killed.

"Major, what's the first thing you're going to do when you get Stateside?" Sergeant Upton asked.

"My brother and I are going to have a beer, rent a car, and drive back to our hometown. Looking forward to a home-cooked meal from our mom."

"Where is home?"

"Wilde, Nevada. There's no place like it on the planet."

Upton nodded. "Like my own Bolivar, Missouri. Home is home."

He wasn't about to correct the man, but Wilde wasn't like anywhere. It was unique in every way. He and Bane had three parents, not because of divorce but because poly families were the norm. Their mom and two dads had returned to Wilde after their sister Shelby's brush with Lily Harris, a deranged woman with blood and revenge in her eyes. Lily was dead and Shelby had found love in the arms of three men from the neighboring town of Elko.

Their other sister, Carolyn, had left town shortly after. He and Bane knew to let Carolyn have her space. She would come around and return to Wilde just as they were doing.

Wilde, Nevada. Home.

Working for the FBI to protect his friends and family from the drug cartel was something he was more than ready to do. It was time to settle down, for both him and Bane. They'd had a great life and had done their duty for the country they loved so much, but they would carry sadness for the men they'd lost in combat to the end of their days. It was time to start the next chapter.

Chapter Two

Emma parked in front of her grandparents' home. Their house sat in the middle of their property, three hundred acres they'd farmed their whole lives. For the past fifteen years, the finest North Dakota land had returned to a more natural state since they'd stop working the farm. It was a beautiful April day with the ground covered in a fresh blanket of snow, late for this time of year.

Her father had been born here. He was her grandparents' only child. He'd broken both their hearts and her mother's.

"Mom, why can't we go with you to Nevada?" Autumn's eyes were wide. "We can help you find a place."

"Honey, I know you want to, but I'm not pulling you out of school. You have your concert coming up." Her daughters were amazing musicians, Autumn playing the violin and Andrea the piano. "Besides, I need to find a job." Em had to believe this change would ease her restless nights and troubled mind. *A new start.* "I know you're going to love Wilde as much as I did when I was your age."

Andrea folded her arms over her chest. "Sure, Mom. Everything was better in the good old days, but what about now?"

"All I'm asking is for you girls to give it a chance." Her grandparents came out on their porch. Their smiles and waves made her feel a little better inside. "Grab your bags, sweethearts. You know you love staying here. Grandma told me on the phone that she baked you each a pie."

"Apple for me, I bet." Autumn grinned from ear to ear. "And chocolate for you, Andrea."

Even her quiet daughter seemed to brighten up some with that news.

Uprooting the girls would be hard on them but Emma didn't feel like she had much of a choice.

A fresh start would do them all good. Andrea and Autumn had been to Wilde on visits and seemed to like the town, but didn't know about living there permanently.

"How're my two favorite angels today?" her grandfather asked her girls. They ran to him, nearly knocking his cane, which was his constant companion since his hip replacement surgery.

"We're great, Grandpa." Autumn held on tight.

"Yes, we are." Andrea let go quickly. Her dour demeanor of disinterest returned, but Emma knew it was more act than reality. Andrea was crazy about her great-grandparents.

"Be careful, girls." Her grandmother gave them both a kiss on their cheeks. "You don't want to knock Grandpa down. I'm not sure we'd be able to get him back up on his feet again."

"Helen, I'm as good as I've ever been." Her grandfather rubbed his white beard. He'd played Santa in town for years and had stopped shaving it off after the New Year's long ago. Father Christmas suited him just fine. "How about I take these little ladies in for some of your delicious pie?"

Andrea's eyes lit up. "Yes. Please."

"Okay, but only little pieces. I don't want to ruin your dinner. We're having fried chicken."

Emma smiled. "Grandma, you shouldn't spoil them so much."

"Hush, Em. They're my great-granddaughters and I love spoiling them rotten." The dear woman turned to her husband. "Take them inside, Leland. It'll give me and Em a chance to talk."

"My pleasure, sweetheart." Grandpa put his arms around her girls and walked into the home Emma's father had grown up in.

"How about we take a load off, child." Grandma walked over to the porch swing and sat down. She patted the seat next to her.

Oh boy. Here it comes.

They sat in silence for several minutes, taking in the view. North

Dakota always looked beautiful, but in the winter, with a fresh layer of snow on the ground, it looked amazing.

She imagined what it was like when her dad had been a child playing in the yard. Much the same, no doubt. North Dakota didn't change, but her father certainly had.

Dad.

Her memories of him were a mixed bag that was filled with happy times and terrible times. He'd suffered with schizophrenia for years. When he was on his meds he'd been amazing. The best times of her life had been in Wilde before her dad had left her mother and returned to North Dakota. His slippery slope had ended tragically. Her grandparents had tried to help him but his delusions had beaten him. He'd stolen a car and at nearly one hundred miles per hour had driven it into a tree in Oak Park, killing him instantly.

"Em, are you sure about moving back to Wilde?"

"Yes." She hated to see tears welling up in her grandmother's eyes.

"Why, honey? Your mom is gone now. Samantha and Lily are, too." Her grandmother had suffered with her son and two granddaughters losing their battles to mental illness. "Family is what matters in these kind of situations. We need to pull together not apart, Em."

"Grandma, I just have been so sad since Mom and Lily's deaths. I miss home."

"This is your home, too."

"I know."

"Please, baby, tell me why. Help me understand this."

She couldn't tell her grandmother the truth. It would crush her. Better to dodge her questions. "You and Grandpa are the only family we have left. We aren't going to stop coming around. A change of scenery will help my girls and me. I've got friends in Destiny. You remember Shelby Taylor."

"I do. She was good to Samantha. I didn't know you two had gotten close though."

Even after all that happened with Samantha and Lily, the town still embraced Emma and somehow that made her feel hopeful. She'd reconnected with Shelby at the funeral, and the sweet woman had continued to call her every day.

Their talks had helped, though she hadn't told even Shelby her worst fears or about the voices she was hearing in the night.

Her grandmother sighed. "Your momma's hometown helped your daddy for a while, baby. It's a good place with good people."

She grabbed her grandmother's hand. "I just need a fresh start. I've always loved Wilde. I'd like to raise my daughters there." There was more to it than that but she wasn't ready to tell her grandmother about her fears of losing her mind. Not now anyway.

"Do you have a job or a place to live?"

"Not yet, but I have some savings. I just need you and Grandpa to watch the girls for me."

"Of course. We love our two little angels. If it doesn't work out the way you want, Em, you can come home. This big house is more than enough for all of us."

A car came up the long driveway. When Emma saw who it was, she felt her shoulders tighten.

Larry, her ex-husband, parked his car.

"Em, you didn't tell him you were leaving, did you?" Her grandmother had never cared for Larry.

She shook her head. "I haven't heard from him in over three months."

"When was the last time he saw the girls?"

"Sometime last year." Her girls didn't have any relationship with him. Emma wished it could be different, but with Larry she doubted it would ever be.

Larry is all about Larry.

"Hey, beautiful ladies." He walked up the steps carrying a box. "Since my girls are here, I bet there's some delicious pie inside, isn't there?"

Before her grandmother could answer, Emma stood up, blocking him from the door. "What are you doing here, Larry?"

"I wanted to see Andrea and Autumn. And I brought their birthday videos back. Thanks for letting me make some copies." He handed her the box.

"How did you know we were here? We haven't seen you in ages."

His infrequent visits always upset her girls. They didn't really know him or trust him. Every time he appeared he came with promises he never kept. In a flash, he disappeared again, staying away for longer and longer periods of time.

"I didn't. I went to your house and when I saw you weren't there, I thought you might be here, at your grandparents' farm."

Her grandmother remained on the porch swing. "Not much of a farm anymore, but it's still home to Leland and me."

Larry smiled. "How is Father Christmas these days, Helen? I heard his surgery went well."

"Not bad for a man who will be eighty-five on his next birthday. There's plenty of pie, Larry." Her grandmother stood. Even though she didn't care for Larry, the woman was always the perfect hostess. "I'll put on a pot of coffee for all of us."

Her grandmother walked inside, leaving Emma and Larry alone on the porch.

"How's your job?" Last she'd heard he still worked in the oil industry, which was booming in the state these days. "You're behind on your child support again."

"Sorry, Emma." He opened up his billfold and pulled out three one hundred dollar bills. "I wish I had never let you go."

"You didn't have a choice, Larry." She'd been the one to end it after all the shit he'd put her through.

"I've just been so busy. Here." He handed her the bills.

"This is hardly enough."

"I'll go to the bank and get you the rest, kitten."

She bristled, hearing him call her the pet name he'd given her years ago.

"I've got a line on something big that will fix all our problems."

"Larry, don't give me your line of bullshit." She took the bills. "Still gambling?"

He shrugged.

Gambling was just one of her ex's vices. The list was long. Cheating. Drinking. Lying. *God, what a fool I was to marry him.* She'd been sixteen, too young to know her own mind. *At least I got two amazing daughters from our marriage.* It had lasted just under two years. Larry had been screwing a neighbor the day Autumn was born. The jerk had missed their daughter's birth entirely.

"Don't make any promises to the girls this time. Please. They've been through enough."

"I heard about your mom and Lily." He extended his arm as if to try to comfort her, but she stepped back.

She didn't want him to ever touch her again. She was willing to be civil with him for the girls, but no more.

He frowned but didn't move forward.

"I'm moving to town, Emma. I will be able to see you and the girls more often. I've been promoted to lead geologist." Larry might not have any common sense when it came to his relationships, but he was quite smart about other things.

Emma wished she didn't have to tell him about the move, but she had to. Larry had visitation rights for Andrea and Autumn, and the court had ordered her to inform him of any changes in address. "We won't be living here much longer."

His face tightened. "Where will you be living?"

"Nevada. We're moving to Wilde."

"Your mom's hometown." Larry shook his head. "I don't think that's a good idea."

"I didn't ask for your opinion. This is my decision." She'd had to learn to become independent. She'd gotten her GED and earned her bachelor's degree. It had been tough with two little ones that depended on her, and she'd done it all on her own. Her ex wasn't about to tell her what to do. Not now. Not ever. "I have full custody of the girls. There is no stipulation in the court papers that says I can't move the girls somewhere else. I only have to let you know our address."

"I guess I deserve that." Larry sighed. "I haven't been the best father to our girls. When are you leaving?"

"First thing in the morning. The girls will be here until I get things settled."

"Not much time to try to rebuild a relationship with them, is it?" He looked troubled.

Was he truly concerned about the girls? Would he actually miss them?

"Emma, I don't want you and the girls to go, but I can understand why you think you should."

He had no clue. He didn't know about the voices at night, about her fear that she would one day lose her mind like both her sisters had. She wished she could trust him, trust anyone with her secrets, but she couldn't.

"I'm going to be better." Larry placed his hand on her shoulder, and this time she didn't pull away. "I messed up, but I want to make it up to you."

"Don't make promises you can't keep."

She had learned a long time ago that her ex always had ulterior motives, always manipulated things and people to his advantage. Had he really changed? Had he finally grown up? She had never loved him and didn't want him in her life, but if he could change for the girls, that would be a dream come true. She didn't know how long she would stay sane. Hopefully this move to Wilde would silence the voices and she could keep her girls, but she just didn't know.

Is it worth the risk to trust him one more time?

Chapter Three

It felt great to be home. Adam had been all around the world but no place held his heart like Wilde.

"What do you think of my new hotel?" Maude Strong was the owner of the Cactus and one of the matriarchs of the town. It had burned down last year.

"It looks amazing. The staircase must've survived the fire."

Maude's two husbands, Greg and Grant, were tending the bar.

"All new, but I told the architect that I wanted an exact replica. He tried to convince me to go another direction, saying it would save money, but he finally came around to my way of thinking."

Bane came up, wearing civilian clothes. "Thanks for this, Maude."

It was quite the party. Round tables, decorated in red, white, and blue filled the space. There was enough delicious food to feed the entire state. Wolfe Mayhem, the band from Destiny, Colorado, played music that kept the dance floor packed. The band's lead singer had the voice of an angel.

Adam turned to their hostess. "Everyone seems to be having a good time."

"All I care about is that *you two boys* are having a good time." She pointed to the banner strung across the back wall with the message *Welcome Home, Adam and Bane, Wilde's Heroes.* "We are all so very proud of you. We're glad to have you home."

He put his arm around the dear lady. "It's good to be home."

"I'm glad your parents finally came back from Australia." Maude motioned to where Mom, Dad Joe, and Papa Bill stood. "Sarah looks so beautiful tonight."

His mom looked like a queen standing between Dad and Pop.

Bane nodded. "I'm glad they had their time down under but this is where they belong."

"Look over there at your sister." Maude pointed to Shelby, who sat with her three husbands, the Champion brothers. Their sister was due any day with her first child. "She's found three great guys to start a family with. I would've never guessed Elko men would marry a Wilde woman, but love can be surprising."

Adam grinned. "Maude, you've always been a hopeless romantic."

"What's wrong with that, soldier?"

"Be careful, bro," Bane said. "She's got you on the ropes."

Maude laughed. "Now, if we can get your sister Carolyn to settle down and move back to town, we'll have the whole Taylor clan where they need to be. Here in Wilde."

"I'd like that, too." His sister Carolyn marched to the beat of her own drum, which often got her into trouble. The whole family knew she'd been looking for something her whole life. He prayed one day Carolyn would find it.

After everyone finished eating, Sheriff Wayne Champion, Shelby's father-in-law, walked over to the wall where the banner hung and clinked his glass. "May I have your attention, please?"

The crowd quieted down.

"Let's have our two guests of honor up here, Adam and Bane Taylor. Join me, soldiers."

Everyone cheered and applauded as he and Bane walked over to the sheriff.

"Four score and seven years ago, the Taylor brothers weren't born yet."

Laughter filled the space.

Sheriff Champion continued, "The good citizens of Wilde are gathered here today to give you a hearty welcome home, and are delighted to have the opportunity to express our full appreciation of the diligent and unwavering service you gave to our country. What you have done in fighting for liberty and freedom around the world has called forth the admiration of Wilde and it is fitting that recognition be made in this way of your valor and patriotic devotion."

Everyone clapped.

"That you have chosen a new profession with the Federal Bureau of Investigation and your home base will be here in our town fills us with such joy and pride."

Another round of applause erupted from the crowd.

Adam grinned, seeing Bane's suffering. His brother, unlike him, didn't care for attention, especially this kind. Most of the details of their service were classified, so their family, friends and neighbors would never know the extent of what they'd accomplished.

"It is my pleasure to present to you Adam Lee Taylor and Bane Joseph Taylor the key to our town." Sheriff Champion handed them an oversized key inscribed with both their names and the date. "From this day forward, the first day in February shall be known as Taylor Brothers Hero Day."

Cheers exploded all around them. "Speech. Speech. Speech."

Adam couldn't help but tease his twin. "You go first."

Bane glared at him. "Fine." He turned to Sheriff Champion. "Thank you, Sheriff and thank you, the wonderful people of Wilde. Does this mean everyone is supposed to give us presents every February first from now on?"

The crowd laughed. Adam smiled, surprised to see Bane moving out of his comfort zone enough to make a joke.

Bane turned to him. "Top that, bro."

Another joke? Wilde seemed to be having quite the impact on his brother, which was good to see.

"Seriously, folks," Bane put his arm around him. "My brother and I are glad to be home. Thank you for this. It means the world to us."

Another round of applause.

"Your turn, Adam."

He scanned the room and saw a gorgeous redhead standing next to

Shelby. She looked familiar but he couldn't quite place her. Not surprising, since he'd been away for so long. Even from this distance he could see the beauty's eyes were a bright green. She had an hourglass shape with full breasts. She was a little taller than most of the women in the room. She was the perfect height for his six-five stature.

"I just want...um..." He never had trouble with public speaking before, but for some reason he couldn't seem to focus. He knew it had something to do with not being able to take his eyes off the beauty next to his sister. "Thank you for this key, Sheriff, but if you really want to make me happy, can you please give me the name and number of that angel standing next to Shelby."

The crowd roared.

* * * *

Emma felt the heat in her face and knew it had to be as red as her hair. She turned to her friend, who was about to become a new mother. "Oh my God, Shelby. I can't believe your brother just said that about me to everyone here."

"Adam is the vocal one, but seeing how Bane is looking at you, I know he's just as interested." Shelby grinned. "You better run or get ready for a double Marine attack from my brothers, Em."

Emma remembered Adam and Bane quite well. Shelby's brothers had been the big men on campus at Wilde High when she had been a freshman. She'd secretly had a crush on them, like every other girl in school. Of course nothing had ever happened between her and the Taylor twins. She'd only been a freshman.

Life after that year had taken a completely different turn. A summer romance while visiting her grandparents' farm had ended in her getting pregnant at sixteen. She'd run off and married Larry, thinking it was the right thing to do, though she'd never loved him. When she'd returned to tell her mother and grandparents, she'd seen the look of concern in their eyes, but they'd still been so loving and supportive of her decision.

"I think running might be the best choice." But before she could turn to seek out the nearest exit, Shelby's two brothers approached her.

"I didn't mean to embarrass you, miss. Permit me to introduce myself. I am Adam Taylor." He grabbed her hand and brought it up to his lips, as if he were from the Victorian age. Just as she remembered him. Adam oozed of charm that was making her weak in the knees.

He and Bane were identical in every way. She even recalled their scam back in school. Adam was better in history and English. Bane was a master at math and science. Since none of the teachers could tell them apart, they would switch classes. They had incredible grades because of the deceit, but were eventually caught and forced to make up all the work.

Devils. Beautiful devils.

I need to remember Adam is wearing the red shirt and Bane the white one.

Six feet five inches of pure muscle. Light brown hair, Marine cut. Dark brown eyes that reminded her of chocolate candy.

"Milady." Bane bowed in front of her, took her other hand, and kissed it just like his twin had done. "How may I make up for my brother's faux pas?"

"That won't be necessary. I was just taken a little aback by the attention." She smiled but wanted to find a quick exit from these overly attractive soldiers. "Again, it was nice seeing you. Thank you for your service to the country. I'm sure you have lots of people who want to talk to you. If you'll excuse me." She turned back to face Shelby.

"Please hold on, miss." Bane touched her elbow, and she felt electricity shoot up her arm. "We didn't even get your name."

"Besides that, this is our party." Adam moved to her other side, offering his arm. "We are the guests of honor. We get to choose who we talk to, and tonight we choose you."

"I can't believe you two don't remember her." Shelby shook her head. "Typical. Guys, this is Emma Harris."

"Emma. Yes. I remember. The cute freshman that just disappeared." Bane's stare gave her a little tremble.

"I remember, too." Adam winked. "So cute. What happened to you? Where did you go?"

She'd never returned to high school, to the two boys whom she continued to dream about until this very day. Now, Adam and Bane Taylor were men, soldiers, standing right next to her. "North Dakota. I got married and had kids."

"Married?" Bane asked, his face clouding with disappointment.

"She's not married now." Shelby seemed to want to play matchmaker. "Hasn't been for over ten years. Maybe the three of you should find a quiet corner and get reacquainted."

"I'm not sure that's a good idea."

"You're right, Emma." Adam smiled. "It's not a good idea. It's a fantastic idea."

Bane nodded. "How about we grab some drinks and sit and talk for a little while."

That does sound wonderful.

Adam and Bane had everything going for them. In another time and another life, she could imagine enjoying their company, but not now. All her focus had to be on finding a job, a place to live, and trying to work on the real issue that had brought her back to Wilde. *The voices.* She'd been in town for two days, and so far, her nights had been quiet and trouble-free. Thank God.

An attractive woman walked over to them. "Hi, Shelby. Sorry to interrupt, but I want to make sure your brothers will give me an interview."

"This is Mackenzie Masters." Shelby seemed to be fond of the woman. "She's the general manager of our television station and the editor of the paper."

"We heard all about you, Mackenzie, from our sister." Bane didn't move away from Emma's side one inch. "Nice to meet you."

Adam nodded. "You're married to Wyatt and Wade, right?"

Emma remembered Wyatt and Wade from high school. The two cowboys were also twins.

"Yes, they're my rough and tumble husbands." Wyatt and Wade, Mac's two husbands, were in another corner talking to some other men. The woman turned to Adam and Bane. "Hey guys, we have a new morning show I'd like to have you on at KINK. What do you say?"

"We really can't talk about our service much. Most of it is classified."

"That's okay. If you come to the station about seven tomorrow morning, we can run through the questions together. Mention some of the places you've been to, the ones not classified. What your plans are going forward in the FBI. That kind of thing. Folks around here love you two. It will make for great television."

"Sure. I always wanted to be a television star." Adam grinned. "Look at this face. It's made for the camera, unlike poor Bane's."

Bane shook his head. "We look exactly the same, bro."

"That's not what my mirror says to me."

They both laughed.

"You two will never grow up." Shelby smiled and turned to Emma and Mackenzie. "Please ignore my brothers. Mac, this is Emma, my friend I was telling you about."

"I thought she might be." Mackenzie extended her hand to Emma. "I understand you are looking for a job."

Emma shook her hand. "Yes. I do need to find something soon." Shelby was turning out to be a very good friend. She'd already been promoting her around town.

"Any background in media or publishing?"

Emma shook her head, worried this chance at a new job would dry up before she got an interview. "I did a couple of journalism classes, but my bachelor's is in business. I've worked several years in banking in North Dakota."

"Banking. Do you like it?"

Actually, she'd found it extremely boring, but it did pay the bills. "Not really," she confessed.

Mac nodded. "I'm in a bit of a bind, Emma. What you don't know, I believe I can teach you. I'd love to talk to you. My new morning show ends at nine tomorrow. Could you come to the station about that time?"

"Yes." Emma felt so excited about this opportunity. Maybe things were really going to turn around for her in Wilde. "Thank you."

"Is that the same show you want us on, Mackenzie?" Bane asked.

The woman nodded. "'Wake Up Wilde' is going to be a local hit, I'm sure."

Bane nodded. "How about we bring Emma with us tomorrow?"

"That will be perfect. Actually, the job I have in mind for her is with the show."

"I don't want to impose." She could tell that Adam and Bane weren't going to give up easily. She had to be careful. She could imagine getting sidetracked completely by the two sweet Marines. "Thank you, but I can drive myself."

Adam put his arm around her shoulders. "You shouldn't deny soldiers who haven't been around a beautiful woman like yourself a chance of buying her breakfast."

Beautiful? He thinks I'm beautiful. She felt her cheeks get quite warm.

"We are not taking 'no' for an answer, Emma. We'll pick you up at six and go to the diner for breakfast." Bane's forceful tone had quite the impact on her, making her tingly inside. "Then we can go to the station together."

She grinned. "You two are used to getting your way, aren't you?"

They both nodded.

"Fine. I surrender to the heroes. I'm staying here at the hotel. I'll meet you at the front at six."

Mackenzie waved at two men Emma didn't recognize. "If you don't mind, I'd like to introduce Emma to Lance and Chuck, the new owners of the paper and television station."

"We don't mind at all, Mac." Shelby gave her a big hug. "Lance and Chuck's wife, Danielle, is part of my girl pack. I can't wait for you to meet all of them."

"You're helping me find a job and find new friends, Shelby. Thank you. I don't know what else to say."

"Don't say anything. You're going to knock everyone's socks off, Em. I'm so glad you're moving back."

"Thanks, Shelby." She turned to Adam and Bane and smiled. "I look forward to tomorrow."

Bane grabbed her hand and kissed it once again. "Our pleasure, Emma."

Adam did the same. "Very much our pleasure."

The two Marines were pulled away by Sheriff Champion and some other attendees.

"I told you to be careful of my brothers, Em." Shelby laughed. "Now you're in trouble. Don't say I didn't warn you."

Shelby's three husbands wrapped her up in their arms. They were Sheriff Champion's sons.

"Honey, how about a dance?" Dr. Alex Champion asked.

Brandon grinned. "With all of us."

"Time to scoot our boots, baby." Justin tipped his hat.

Alex grabbed Shelby's hands. "We promise to not get carried away, sweetheart. Just slow and easy."

Shelby shook her head and smiled. "Doctor, is this your way of trying to get me to go into labor?"

"It couldn't hurt."

"Maybe you should go talk to Charly and her guys about hitting the dance floor. She's past the due date you gave her, too."

"The whole town is on pins and needles about when these two newest citizens will be born," Mackenzie said. "You know there's a pool. I've got tonight at 11:30 p.m. for Charly and tomorrow at 4:00 a.m. for you, Shelby."

"I'll see if I can help you win something, Mac, but it's going to be more walking than dancing." Shelby looked lovingly at her three guys. "I will not be soaking my feet tomorrow. The last time we all went dancing you kept me out on the floor all night. Three songs. That's all I am up to, okay?"

"Three is perfect, baby." Justin kissed his bride on the cheek.

Shelby groaned and grimaced. Looking into her friend's face, Emma thought she might be having a contraction.

Justin frowned. "I didn't know my kisses had that kind of impact on you, sweetheart."

Brandon touched Shelby's shoulders. "Honey?"

Concerned for Shelby, Emma asked, "Did you just have a contraction?"

Shelby shrugged. "Probably just Braxton Hicks."

"Doc. Doc." Dax Strong, one of Charly's husbands, ran up to them. "My wife's water just broke."

Alex turned to Brandon and Justin. "I'm going to go check on Charly, but we're not taking any chances with our Shelby. Keep an eye on her. She might be right about it being false labor, but if anything changes, bring her to the hospital." He and Dax left in a sprint for Charly.

Justin and Brandon asked Shelby questions about how she was feeling and did she need to sit down. Shelby smiled and told them she was fine. Her words didn't take away the concern in the two men's faces.

Emma thought it was great how her friend's husbands were taking care of her.

Shelby closed her eyes and moaned.

Mac grabbed Shelby's hand. "That's another contraction, no doubt."

Justin lifted Shelby up in his arms. "We're going to the hospital right now, baby."

"I'll let Alex know she's had another contraction and we're taking her to the hospital." Brandon ran to the men around Charly.

In a flash, all the fathers to be rushed Shelby and Charly out of the party to the new Wilde Hospital. Adam and Bane, the uncles to be, left with their parents to go to the waiting room. The majority of the crowd followed. The few remaining were abuzz with excitement for the two families. Everyone would be heading to the hospital to wait for the new babies to arrive.

Emma turned to Mackenzie. "What a night."

"Shelby and Charly are going to be wonderful mothers, Em." Something about Mackenzie's tone told her the woman would make a great mom, too.

"Thank you for considering me to work with you."

"I'll be the one thanking you. I sure need help. Lots of changes coming in the next several months." Mackenzie was glowing. Was she pregnant? "I might be able to have dinner with my husbands now. Let's go talk to the big bosses."

She walked with Mac to meet the owners.

Life was already looking brighter.

Chapter Four

Bane glanced around the waiting room. The hospital still had quite the crowd, though some had to leave for their shifts in the Wilde Silver Mine. Of those remaining, most had nodded off, but not his parents. They were wide awake, sitting in the chairs closest to the swinging doors that led to the delivery room.

"Look at Mom and Dads, bro." He sat in the waiting room with Adam, anxiously anticipating the arrival of Shelby's baby. "You think they'd like something to eat?"

His brother shook his head. "Nope. I just asked them less than fifteen minutes ago. They told me they are too excited to eat. I'm in the same boat."

"Me, too." Bane grinned and looked at the clock—*zero-four-hundred.* He recalled one mission where he had been cut off from his unit. Being behind enemy lines and under heavy fire, he hadn't been able to eat for forty-eight hours. This should be a piece of cake. "Food after Shelby's baby comes, and not before."

"Agreed," Adam said.

An hour ago, Charly had delivered a healthy baby boy. Gregory Grant Strong was named after his grandfathers on his dads' side. The little cowboy had arrived twenty and a half inches long and weighed eight pounds four ounces. All the Strong brothers and their parents were with Charly and the new baby.

Emma and Mackenzie returned from the nursery and sat down across from them.

Bane couldn't keep his eyes off of Emma. *God, she's gorgeous.*

"Charly's baby boy is so handsome." Emma smiled, making her

appear even more beautiful. "Does Shelby know if her baby is a boy or girl?"

"She's having a girl, though she and her guys haven't told anyone what the baby's name is going to be." He loved Emma's flowing red hair and full lips. Her green orbs enthralled him. Her porcelain, delicate skin enticed him. But it was more than just her body that drew him in. She was direct, thoughtful, kind, open, and so very sweet. All the traits his deepest self responded to.

Emma was the ideal woman, perfect in every way.

Mac looked at the time on her cell. "I lost Charly's pool and it's after four, so I didn't win Shelby's either. I wonder who did win. That would be a cute interview for the morning show."

"Will you have to bump these two heroes?" Emma asked. She and Mac had clearly hit it off, talking about all kinds of things throughout the night.

"I know they will not leave until Shelby delivers her baby, that's for sure." Mac glanced down at the time again. "I'm going to have to head to the studio pretty quick. God, I hate to leave. I want to stay for Wilde's newest citizen's arrival, too."

"I've got an idea, Mac," Emma said. "Why not shoot your show right here in the waiting room? You could still interview Bane and Adam and get the other big story in town front and center. Charly and Shelby's babies."

Mac smiled. "I love that idea. Done. I'm going to call the guys and get a crew over here ASAP. You're a natural, Em. I just knew you would be. If you want the job, it's yours. Assistant Program Director. We can work out all the terms later."

Emma took her hand. "Yes. I want the job. Thank you, Mac. Thank you so much."

"Let me make the call. I want you by my side during the show, okay?"

"Absolutely. I'm really excited about this opportunity." Emma's enthusiasm was endearing. "I won't let you down."

"I know you won't. We're going to make quite the team, Em. If we're lucky, Shelby will deliver the baby during the show." Mac laughed and walked to a quiet corner to make her call.

"I know you two are very excited about being uncles." Emma leaned forward. "That sweet, little baby will never want for anything as long as you two are around. Your family sure does pull together, don't they?"

Bane nodded, though he wondered why Carolyn had yet to show up. Of his two sisters, he never did understand her. Carolyn had been troubled her entire life. One day, he prayed she would find peace and happiness.

Who am I to complain about siblings? He looked at Emma, whose two sisters had been homicidal crazy women. They were dead, as was her mother. Emma had been through hell and back.

"Do you have boys or girls, Em?" Adam asked.

Bane recalled she'd mentioned having children earlier.

"Two girls." Her entire face beamed with pride. "Twelve and thirteen. Autumn and Andrea."

He was glad she wasn't completely alone in the world. "Do you have pictures of them?"

"On my phone." She brought out her cell and showed him and Adam a picture of the two girls.

Adam took the phone from her. "They are so cute, Em." His brother handed him the cell. "Don't you agree, Bane?"

"I sure do." He turned to Emma. "They look a lot like you. They both have your eyes and your gorgeous red hair."

"I know, but they are much prettier than me. They take after my sisters that way." Her words didn't sit well with him. Didn't she know she was gorgeous? "Thankfully, they don't look a thing like their father."

When Emma mentioned her ex, Bane saw a slight frown appear on her face that didn't sit well with him. It was clear that she didn't want to talk about the man, which suited him just fine. "After Shelby has the baby and we finish with the television show, let's go to breakfast, Em."

"We're all going to be starving by then." Adam obviously was into Emma as much as he was. A first date was exactly what they needed. And a second. And a third.

"Guys, I'm just getting settled. I've only been in town for a short time. I think I'll head back to the hotel for some much-needed sleep. You two should do the same. You have to be exhausted after your party last night and this long wait on your sister to deliver the baby."

"Shelby has always made us wait, but she's worth it." Adam took Emma's hand. "I know you're tired but you have to eat, Em. A full tummy will help you sleep better."

"I've always heard if you eat before you sleep you can have nightmares." She grinned.

Bane joined in on the teasing. "So let's put it to the test. You can report back to us for dinner tonight if our breakfast upsets your dreams."

"That's two meals you're trying to lock me down for." Smiling, she shook her head. "Quite the two operators, aren't you?"

"You have no idea, sweetheart." Adam leaned back and rubbed his chin, a sure sign he thought he was about to win a date with Emma. "What will your new boss think if we refuse to go on camera this morning?"

"That's blackmail, Adam Taylor."

"Bane and I want to go on a date with you, Emma. We will resort to whatever is necessary to get that chance."

"You might as well give up, Em. Adam sure isn't going to. And neither am I. One date. That's all." But he knew one date with her would never be enough. Still, it was a start.

"Guys, can't we just be friends?"

He wasn't about to let her off the hook. "Friends go to breakfast together, don't they?"

"I suppose they do."

Winking, he asked, "Then your answer is...?"

"Fine. Breakfast." Her surrender was one of the sweetest he'd ever received. "Just breakfast. Okay?"

Before he or Adam could answer, Alex came through the swinging doors.

"I'm a dad. I have the most beautiful daughter in the world. She looks like her amazing mother."

The crowd erupted in cheers.

Bane turned to Adam. "We're uncles, bro."

Adam slapped him on the back. "Yes we are."

Shelby and Grace Madelyn Champion are doing great." The new father looked happier than Bane had ever seen him before. "We'll have my new baby girl in the nursery in about fifteen minutes."

Emma smiled. "Congratulations, guys."

Caught up in the happy moment, Bane pulled her into his arms and squeezed her tight. "I am an uncle. Wow."

"Don't forget about me. I'm an uncle, too." Adam kissed Emma on the cheek. "It's a big job, but don't you think me and my brother will be good at it?"

She laughed. "You two will be the best uncles on the planet."

"Emma, make sure nobody moves a muscle." Mac held up her hand. "You're all going to be on KINK's morning show."

* * * *

Emma sat between Bane and Adam at the diner named after her mother. The new owner hadn't changed a thing, which pleased her very much. Norma's held a million good memories for her. She'd grown up here. Her mom started her and her sisters at very young ages washing dishes and busing tables. Emma smiled remembering a food fight with her sisters when her mom had stepped out for a moment. They'd had to clean up the place fast before their mother returned.

What ever happened to my sisters? Samantha and Lily had been so different when they were younger.

"Want some more coffee, Em?" Bane's thoughtfulness was sweet. He and Adam had been so attentive.

"No. I'm stuffed." She looked at her empty plate. "I can't believe I ate so much. I sure have missed King Cakes." King Cakes were actually fluffy pancakes that had been named years ago after an unscheduled stop by Elvis Presley to town. She glanced over at the familiar signed menu and photo of the King sitting at Norma's bar. It hung on the wall behind the cash register.

Adam put his arm around her shoulders. "There's nothing like them anywhere else."

"That's for sure."

"You did a terrific job this morning, Em." Bane pushed his plate to the side. "Being Assistant Program Manager fits you to a tee."

She'd enjoyed working with Mackenzie so very much. "It was easy because you guys were great on the show."

"We were good, weren't we?" Adam laughed. "You are both right—we were good and Emma was great—but I think the main reason the show was a success was because of Grace Madelyn."

"And we best not forget Gregory Grant, Adam." Emma remembered how wonderful it had been to hold her two daughters for the first time and was certain the new mothers were feeling the same for their babies. "Gregory with his coal-black hair and Grace with her blonde hair."

As if on cue, Maude, Greg, and Grant Strong walked into the diner.

Maude spotted them. "There you are, Emma." The trio headed to their table.

Emma had known the Strongs her whole life. They were so happy together. "Congratulations. How does it feel to be grandparents to the cutest baby boy on the planet?"

"Feels amazing," Greg answered.

Grant nodded. "Congratulations, fellas. Your niece is so precious." "Those two darling bundles stole the show, didn't they, Emma?" Maude sat down across from them.

"They sure did."

Maude's charisma was endearing. "I don't want to interrupt, but I wanted to ask you something. Is it true that you're looking for a place to live?"

"Yes. I'm moving back here, and I want a place for my girls and me."

Maude reached across the table and grabbed her hands. "That makes me so happy. I love my new hotel and hope you are enjoying your stay, but you need something more permanent. I have a rental house that I think would be perfect for you. Three bedrooms and two baths. It even has a garage. It's on Windfall Street just a block away from the middle school."

"Maude that would be fantastic. When can I see it?"

"Anytime, sweetie."

"Would this evening be okay? I need some sleep."

Maude nodded. "I think we all do. Let's say about five."

"Perfect." She loved how everyone in this town took care of each other.

"I miss Norma so much. She was such a great friend to me. She would be thrilled that you are moving back." Maude squeezed her hands. "Wilde is your home. You belong here."

"Honey, let's get our breakfast." Greg winked. "I think these three might need more time alone."

Emma shook her head. "We're about to leave, Mr. Strong. This was only breakfast with friends."

"Uh-huh." The new grandpa smiled and sent her another wink.

Adam stood and held out his hand. "After we take you to look at the house, Em, we really need your help to find a present for the most perfect little niece in the world."

Bane's smile gave her a little tingle. "And don't forget we need presents for little Gregory and his mom and Shelby, too."

Maude grinned. "Sounds like you three will have to spend a lot of time together. Shopping can be quite a chore."

"We are just two old Marines, Maude. We need Emma's help." Adam's warm gaze unhinged her. "What do you say, Em? Will you help us out?"

How can I refuse them? "Okay. Shopping after I look at Maude's rental house. As friends."

"Uh-huh," Bane and Adam said in unison, but she knew by the looks on their faces they were hoping for more.

The Strongs went to another booth to order their breakfast.

Feeling the fatigue of staying up all night, Emma yawned. "I'm sorry."

"Nothing to be sorry about, Em. Time to get you back to your room." Clearly, Adam meant to walk her to the hotel.

Bane yawned. "Your yawning is contagious. I think we all could use a few hours of shut-eye."

"We're on the same page." Adam yawned. "It's really contagious. Let's go before we all fall asleep right here."

She walked between Adam and Bane to the new Hotel Cactus. The old one had been destroyed in a fire. They entered the lobby, which was even more grand than the former one had been. As they headed up the stairs to her room, she felt her heart start to race. Why? They were only acting in a gentlemanly manner walking her to her door. Nothing more. She was being silly.

When they got to her room, she turned to them. "Thank you for breakfast and escorting me back here. What time will you pick me up?"

"A quarter to five." Bane leaned in and kissed her gently.

"Don't forget, shopping after we look at Maude's house, Em." Adam tenderly pressed his lips to hers.

Her legs were weak. *Is it from their kisses or from being so tired?* But she knew it was from their kisses. "Good night. Wait. It's morning. Let me say until later." She opened her door.

Bane hugged her. "Later for sure, Em."

"Bye, sweetheart." Adam touched her cheek.

Then the two Marines turned and headed down the stairs.

She went into her room and shut the door.

She stripped off her clothes and leaned back on the bed.

Her eyes were heavy because she was feeling so relaxed at all the wonderful prospects in front of her. Things were looking up for her and her girls.

She was about to drift off when her cell buzzed.

"Damn. I just want some sleep." She slid her finger across the screen. "Hello?"

"You thought you could get away from us by going back to Wilde, Emma, darlin'."

Lily?

Every inch of her body stiffened. "Lily, is that really you?"

Instead of Lily answering her, Samantha's voice came through the speaker. "You were wrong, Em. We're still coming for you."

"Sam? Why are you doing this to me?"

The line went dead.

Trembling, she tossed the phone to the floor. The voices were back.

How is this happening? Lily and Samantha are dead.

Gathering her wits, she grabbed her cell and looked at the screen to see where the call originated. What she saw filled her with dread. *Unknown.*

Was that an actual call or am I going crazy? There was no way she would be able to sleep now. She hoped a hot bath would relax her, but she doubted it would work. She couldn't stop thinking about the phone call. *There has to be an answer to why this is happening to me.*

Chapter Five

Adam parked his truck in front of the Hotel Cactus. "We're here."

"Right on time, too." Bane jumped out of the cab, clearly as anxious as he was to get back to Emma.

He felt refreshed, in part from the few hours of sleep they'd been able to get, but mostly from anticipation of seeing Emma again.

They entered the lobby and saw her sitting on one of the plush sofa's gazing at her cell phone.

"God, isn't she the most gorgeous woman you've ever seen, Bane?"

"Damn right, she is. And her beauty isn't just on the outside, bro. It runs through all of her." Bane was absolutely right about Emma.

They were both thrilled to be spending time with such an amazing woman.

"Bane, she's not even aware we are here, is she?"

"She doesn't seem to be. Obviously, she's lost in thought about something."

As they got closer, they could see her beautiful eyes had tears starting to overflow. Realizing she was upset about something concerned him. Though they'd only just met, he had a strong urge to hold and comfort her.

He and Bane rushed to Emma.

They glanced at her cell and saw the pictures of her dead sisters on her screen. She had suffered so many losses and was obviously struggling with her grief.

Emma looked up at them, quickly wiping her eyes. "You're here already."

He sat down on one side of her and took her hand. Bane moved to the other side, putting his arm around her shoulders.

"We understand that you're sad, Em." He squeezed her delicate hand.

Bane jumped in. "Would you like to get a drink before we leave?"

Believing she needed to open up to heal, he added, "Or we could go somewhere private to talk if you like."

"I appreciate your concern, but I'd rather just go if you don't mind." She stood and shoved her cell into her purse.

He realized she wasn't ready to talk about what was troubling her. "Emma, whatever you need is what we'll do."

"Thank you, but I don't want to be late. Maude is expecting me."

* * * *

As they turned onto Windfall, Emma saw Maude's truck parked in front of the cutest house on the block. The outside was so eye catching with its large trees and beautiful landscaping. She could tell it had been very well taken care of. "I hope the inside is as nice as the outside."

"Knowing Maude, I'm sure it is." Adam parked his truck next to Maude's.

Bane got out from the back and opened her door. "Ready to take a look at your new place, Em?"

She nodded.

The three of them walked up to the pretty porch that wrapped around the entire front and sides. The door opened, revealing Maude.

"I heard you drive up. Come on inside, Emma. I think you will love this place."

She walked inside and realized how perfect this home would be for her and her girls. It was gorgeous. "Maude, this is amazing. I love the open floor plan, and the kitchen with all the stainless steel appliances is a dream. I'm just not sure I can afford something this elaborate."

Maude smiled. "You've only taken a single step into the house, Em. Let's go see the rest of it. Okay?"

She turned to Bane and Adam. "Would you mind looking at the place with me guys? I would appreciate your opinion." *Why did I say that?*

Bane nodded.

"Absolutely," Adam answered.

She'd been on her own for years, handling everything herself. Still, it was nice to have these two Marines by her side to at least ask their advice.

They walked around the home that was perfect in every way. Andrea and Autumn would have their own rooms, which were each double the size of the one they shared in North Dakota. The Master had a sitting room and a giant en suite with separate shower and garden tub.

Maude turned to her after showing her the backyard, which was lined with stunning red rose bushes. "So, Em? What do you think? Will this work for you?"

"Maude, it's amazing. I wouldn't change anything. It's my style in every way. The colors. The layout. Everything. It's just not going to fit my budget. Maybe later. But for now I should probably get an apartment at Wilde Oaks."

"I always wait for the right person to rent my houses to, Em. I want someone I know I can trust. When I first found out that you needed a home, I knew that would be you." Maude reached in her purse and pulled out some paperwork and a set of keys. "Money doesn't concern me one bit, young lady. Here's the lease. Will this fit your budget?"

Emma looked at the agreement. Maude had already typed in her name and a price that was about the same as she was paying for the two-bedroom apartment in North Dakota. "Maude, this is too low. I just couldn't."

"Oh yes you can. Now sign." Maude pulled out a pen and handed it to her. "I know you love it."

Adam put his arm around her shoulders. "I think you've been overruled, Em."

She signed the lease and hugged Maude. "I don't know what to say, but thank you so much."

"No. I'm thanking you. I can sleep at night knowing my house is well taken care of. Who knows, you might want to buy it someday for you and the girls." Maude grinned and looked over at Bane and Adam. "It's big enough for an entire family, you know."

Emma loved the dear woman, but she made her blush.

Maude turned back to her. "Here are the keys. I've got to get back to my grandson and my daughter-in-law. Doc is releasing them in an hour and I want to be there."

Emma took the keys. "The lease doesn't start until the first of next month."

"Don't start with me, young lady. It's yours. Lock up when you leave." Maude addressed Bane and Adam. "Take good care of my renter, boys. Bye."

After her sweet landlady walked out the door, Emma turned to Bane and Adam. "I've just got to walk around this house one more time, guys. Do you mind? I just can't believe this is mine." She felt better than she had all day. Things were looking up again.

As they walked around with her, she told them how she would decorate each room. "My mother's buffet would look wonderful on this wall. I'm just so excited. I can't wait to get my girls here and start our new life. Are you guys hungry? Do you mind if we grab a bite before we go shopping?"

"My sentiments exactly," Bane said. "We haven't eaten since breakfast."

"How about we go to the steakhouse?" Adam asked.

"I didn't know there was a steakhouse in Wilde."

"We've all been away too long, Em." Bane pulled her in close.

"But Shelby told us the food at Reno Steakhouse is mouthwatering. It's on the highway five miles north of The Masters' Chambers."

* * * *

"I can't remember when I had so much fun." Bane held Emma's hand as they walked into the Hotel Cactus.

"Me either," she said. "I love spending someone else's money."

"I never cared for shopping before, but you made it fun, Em." Adam laughed. "I especially liked the onesie you tried on for Shelby."

Emma smiled. "She's going to love the selfie we took of the three of us in pajamas."

"How many stores did you run us through?" Bane wiped his brow, overemphasizing his fatigue. "You wore us out."

She shrugged. "How many stores are in the county?"

"We saw them all." Bane wanted to spend more time with this amazing woman. Much more time. He grinned. "It's going to take a week to work out these knots in my calves."

"And you call yourself Marines? You should see me around Christmastime. This was just a little sprint compared to that marathon."

"Haven't you ever heard of online shopping?" Adam shook his head and slumped into one of the sofas in the lobby. "If you ever want to try out basic training, sweetheart, I'm sure you would pass with flying colors."

"Most mothers of two teenagers would." Emma laughed, a sound he wanted to hear again and again and again. She landed next to Adam on the sofa.

Looking at her and his brother, something profound hit Bane square in the face. She was the one they'd been searching the world for, the one who would change everything for the better for them, the one they would build a life and a future together with.

I want her. She's the one for us.

"Oh God. I have to stop laughing, guys. I'm still so full from our dinner."

"Shelby was right about the steaks at Reno." Adam put his arm around Emma. "Our meal was so delicious and satisfying."

She nodded. "Thank you. I needed this evening more than you know."

Bane sat down next to her, placing her between him and Adam, right where she belonged. "Baby, you're the real reason it was a perfect night."

Her green eyes sparkled. "I could say the same about you and Adam."

He leaned in and kissed her, tasting the sweetness of her lips. Every possessive cell inside him came alive as he deepened their kiss sending his tongue into her delicious mouth. He inhaled her breaths, claiming even them as his own. His heart thudded like a hammer in his chest.

When he released Emma, her face was beautifully flushed.

Her lips parted, but before she could say anything, Adam kissed her. She placed her delicate hands on his brother's shoulder. When Adam ended their kiss, Emma's breathing was labored, causing her breasts to heave.

As their kissing intensified, his own hunger burned for satiation. He needed to keep control, but something dangerous and famished had been unleashed inside him. His need to possess and to conquer thundered inside him.

He stroked her hair. "I think I should go get us a bottle of wine and we take this to your room, if that's okay with you, Em?"

"I don't want this evening to end yet, and I'm not ready to be alone. So, yes. I think it's a very good idea."

Her words were music to his ears. "Why don't you walk her up to her room, Adam, and I'll be there just as soon as I get the wine."

His brother stood. "My pleasure, bro."

"Red or white, Em?"

"White."

Adam grabbed her hand to help her stand.

Bane smiled, watching them as they headed up the stairs. He walked to the bar. The bartender gave him a bottle of the best white wine they had in stock and three wine glasses. He bolted up to the second floor. Like Em, he was not ready for the evening to end.

We might even watch the sun rise together.

He walked into her hotel room, which was quite lavish by most standards. Not surprising since all the rooms in the Cactus were palatial. When Maude had rebuilt the hotel, she'd spared no expense.

He sat the bottle on the table. "I forgot to ask for an opener. Damn."

Emma smiled. "No worries. There's one by the ice bucket. This room seems to have everything you would ever need. There's even a ton of movies on Blu-ray. Would you guys like to watch one?"

Adam put his arm around her. "Maybe later, but for now let's just enjoy our wine and talk."

Bane completely agreed with his brother. He wanted to get to know Emma even more.

She nodded. "That sounds perfect to me."

He opened the bottle and poured each of them a glass. "Here you go, sweetheart."

"Thank you." She took it and brought it up to her lush lips.

After lots of conversation and laughter and finishing off their drinks, Bane saw her cheeks were a bright red, indicating she was warm and having a good time.

Adam downed the last drop of the wine. "All gone. Should I head down to the bar for another bottle, Em?"

"No thank you." She smiled. "I'm fine. Actually more than fine."

God, I love the sound of that. Bane looked at his watch. "It's oh-two hundred."

"Two in the morning? It's still early." She clearly wasn't ready to be alone. "Any ideas of what we can do next? Do you like games? I saw a deck of cards in one of the drawers of the dresser. How about poker?"

Adam raised one eyebrow. "What are the stakes, Em?"

He knew exactly where his brother was headed to give them an advantage. The two of them were masters at manipulating the cards thanks to a love of magic tricks when they were teenagers.

"I've got some change in my purse. It would just be for fun."

Adam grinned. "I know what is really fun. Strip poker."

She giggled. "Seriously?"

He'd never wanted a woman more than he wanted Emma right now. "Now that's a game I could get into."

"Oh really?" She got up and pulled out the deck of cards. She came back to the table and shuffled them expertly. "You two better reconsider. I'm quite good at poker. If you're not careful, you'll both be walking out of this room naked."

"Oh. That's really a challenge." He and Adam were pretty good at poker when they played fair. When they chose to use sleight of hand, they were extraordinary and unbeatable, not that they ever cheated in any real game. It was always just fun, but tonight he knew would make all those other times seem dull and boring. Tonight, with Emma, would be amazing. He and Adam needed to throw out all the stops. "Waving the red flag in front of us, are you?"

"You bet." Her grin nearly drove him mad with desire. "Would one of you like to cut?"

He nodded and picked up half the deck, placing it underneath the rest of the cards. His old magic skills were still intact, as Emma didn't notice that he'd palmed several cards when he brought his hand back and placed it under the table.

"Here are the rules." Emma's confidence was evident. "Five card stud. The winner of the hand decides who takes off a piece of clothing."

Adam nodded. "Pretty sure of yourself, sweetheart, aren't you?"

"Just wait and see, fellas. Wait and see." She dealt the cards.

He turned to Adam, who gave him a knowing look. Let her win a couple of hands first. *Perfect.*

"Three sevens." She smiled broadly. "I win. Told you."

"Damn," they both said in unison, trying to hold back their laughter.

"Bane, take off your boots."

"Wait a second, Miss Card Shark." He loved her smugness. "Shouldn't it only be one boot?"

"Fine. Take off your left boot."

He took it off and tossed it to the side. "My deal."

He shuffled the cards, making sure she had the winning hand again.

"A full house. I'm on fire. Adam, take off your left shoe."

"Shit." Adam turned to him. "We might be in real trouble with this one."

It was all part of the ruse and it was working perfectly. The four hands they'd let her win had given her a confident laughter that was contagious.

Time to turn the tables on you, baby. "Give me the cards, Em."

"If you two want to call it quits, I would understand completely. You are outgunned."

"Are we? I feel lucky." He dealt the cards, giving her three Kings but Adam three Aces.

"How about we raise the stakes, boys?" She'd taken the bait just like he thought she would.

He was having the time of his life. "What did you have in mind, sweetheart?"

"Two pieces for this hand."

"She must have a killer hand if she's wanting to raise." Adam was laying it on thick, and it was working perfectly. "I may be making a big mistake, but how about three?"

"Too rich for my blood." He folded his hand.

Her eyes narrowed. "Really, Adam? I can tell you're bluffing."

"Call or fold, Em."

"I call. Read 'em and weep, boys. Three Kings. Adam, take off your shirt."

"A little premature, baby." His brother placed his winning hand on the table. "Three Aces beats Kings, don't they?"

She shook her head. "I can handle one lucky hand. I've got both shoes and my ring. I'm still in good shape."

"You've got the best shape I've ever seen." Bane touched her cheek.

"And we're going to get to see more of it, too," Adam teased. "Take off your shoes and ring, Em. I won."

She obeyed beautifully, placing her discarded items on the floor next to her. "Whose deal is it?"

"My turn." Adam shuffled the cards.

After his brother dealt, Bane looked at his hand. A Jack-high flush. He wasn't sure what Adam had given Emma, but he knew it had to be a lesser hand than his. "I'm thinking we should up the stakes again."

She looked at her hand and nodded. "Tough guy, huh?"

"You bet, sweetheart."

"Well, my luck disappeared." Adam pushed his cards to the side. "I fold."

"I warn you, Bane. I've got you beat." She placed her cards face down in front of her. "Let's see what you're made of. Four pieces, soldier. What do you think about that?"

"Are you so sure, Em?" He winked. "How about five?"

"Mmm. I count a pair of socks, a shirt, jeans, and a watch. That'll leave you in your underwear."

"Honey, I go commando."

Her eyes widened and her cheeks turned a pretty shade of pink.

"I count on you your earrings, your blouse, and your slacks. That'll leave you in your bra and panties, if you dare to call."

She picked up her cards from the table and stared long and hard at them. "Five? Okay. I call."

"I hope this is the best hand." He sighed, adding to her suffering. She squirmed and leaned forward. "Well?"

"I might've made a big mistake."

"Just show your cards. Please."

"Okay. Okay." He laid them down one at a time. "Here's a three of hearts, a five of hearts, an eight of hearts, a ten of hearts and…a Jack of hearts."

"Oh my God." Her hand came up to her mouth. "I can't believe it."

"That's what I have, Em. It's right in front of your eyes. I've got a flush. What do you have, sweetheart?"

"Not enough. A big hand though." She showed him the King high straight. "You win."

Chapter Six

Emma felt a warm shiver run up and down her spine. Bane and Adam's sexy eyes locked in on her. She unfastened her earrings slowly, anxious and excited. It had been years since she'd been in nothing but her bra and panties in front of anyone, let alone a man. Now, she was about to be in front of two men, two gorgeous men, two Marines.

"Would you like some help, sweetheart?" Bane's tone deepened, rumbling from within his muscled chest.

"Yes, please."

Adam leaned over and kissed her and Bane stroked her hair, making her toes curl. Adam traced her lips with his tongue and Bane feathered her shoulder with his hot manly lips.

She'd grown up in Wilde. Being with two men wasn't unusual. In fact, it was the norm here. She'd come home looking for some peace and had found Bane and Adam. With their caresses and kisses moving over her body, she felt so alive and on fire.

"There's still the matter of our wager, sweetheart." Bane pressed his lips to hers, which were throbbing deliciously.

He and Adam helped her to her feet. They slowly stripped her of her clothes, leaving her in only her bra and panties.

They stepped back and stared at her. Their gazes told her they approved of what they saw.

"Em, think of a card."

"What?"

His eyes were filled with mischievousness. "Think of a card. Now."

"Okay. Jack of clubs."

"Oh. I'm sorry. I win. I was thinking of the Queen of hearts." He smiled. "I guess I'll have to remove your bra."

"Hey, I was thinking of the Queen of hearts, too." Bane grinned wickedly. "She owes me her panties."

She laughed, thrilled at their amusing taunting. "You two don't play fair, do you?"

"Never." Adam moved behind her and unclasped her bra. He pulled the straps off her shoulders and removed the garment. He cupped her breasts with his hands. "Not when it comes to something we want."

"And you, Em, we want more than anything." Bane knelt down, tracing his fingers down her side, sending a flood of warmth through her body. He gently removed her panties. "God, you are gorgeous."

This feels so good and so right.

Bane moved his hands back up her legs, urging her with only his touch to part her thighs for him.

At first, she resisted, but as he massaged her legs, she slowly relaxed. His fingers found her slick folds and brushed her moistness. Her breath caught in her chest and her heartbeat went into overdrive.

Oh, God! I need this. I need to lean on their strength, at least for tonight. I want to escape the voices and myself. Yes. I want this.

Without a word, they placed her face up on the bed. They stepped back, their eyes fixed on her.

Adam stripped off his clothes, revealing his chiseled chest and six-pack abs. He pulled out a couple of packages of condoms from the pocket of his jeans, handing one to Bane.

Their hot gazes burned her up to the core, threatening to melt her insides. Her need to be claimed by them, to have their mouths devouring hers, to surrender her body to them, scorched her, leaving her deliciously dizzy.

"My God, Emma, you are perfect." Bane removed his shirt and jeans. The two men were mirror images of each other in every department. She couldn't help but look between their legs. Their long, thick cocks were erect.

"So are you and Adam. In every way."

Bane and Adam moved onto the bed, one on each side of her. They caressed her gently, each massaging a breast. Adam pinched her nipple, delivering a sweet sting, as Bane kissed her deeply. Tingles started swirling inside her. Their touches were overwhelming. Lost to her desire, she reached down and took hold of their cocks, which were massive and warm.

"Yes, baby. That feels so good." Adam growled.

"Squeeze our cocks." Bane kissed her neck, delivering a delicious shiver throughout her body. "Tighten your pretty little hands around our shafts."

She obeyed, rubbing her hands over the head of their cocks. She felt the slipperiness of their tiny liquid pearls on the tips of her fingers. Her need to have them inside her body grew and grew.

Bane placed one of his hands over hers, slowing her strokes on his dick, and moved the other one to her pussy. He threaded his thick fingers through her swollen, dampening folds. Her pussy ached and her clit began to throb. Adam swallowed her nipple, capturing the tingling bit of flesh between his teeth.

She didn't realize that sex could be so wonderful. Bane and Adam were tender, forceful, and attentive. She was amazed how her body was responding to them, reacting to their touches on so many levels. Heat rolled through her and she squeezed her legs together, trying to find relief from the growing pressure, but none came.

She'd never experienced real release. Would she climax tonight? *Could I actually have an orgasm?* With Bane and Adam, she thought she might.

Bane shifted down the bed, coming up between her legs. She could feel the heat of his breath on her pussy. He grabbed her legs and placed them on his shoulders.

Oh God. No man has ever done this to me before.

He kissed her inner thighs, and she got even wetter.

She wanted his mouth on her pussy, needed his most intimate kiss there. "Please, Bane. Please."

Adam laved her nipples until they were throbbing like mad. "Baby, keep begging like that and you'll get anything you want."

"Nice and wet with sweet cream." Bane sent his tongue through her moist folds, licking her into a state of delirium.

Her body had never felt like this before, so on fire. She lifted her hips off the mattress, needing to feel more of his hungry mouth on her pussy.

"You're so fucking hot, baby." Adam reached under her and fingered her ass.

"Oh God. Oh yes. God. So good." Her breaths were so shallow, coming faster and faster. The pressure grew and grew.

Bane continued lapping up her juices, driving her to the edge of sanity.

"That's it, baby." Adam's hands and mouth expanded the crushing need inside her. "You're almost there."

Suddenly, she reached a peak she'd never experienced before. Every cell tingled in her body.

Something amazing occurred, something she'd only imagined, something she'd believed would never be hers.

It's happening. Oh God. I'm having an orgasm. Oh my God, so this is what it feels like.

Her entire body united into a giant explosion of release. Shivering sensations shot through her, and her pussy began to spasm again and again. She clawed at Bane's shoulders, lost to the climax he and Adam had given her.

She had uncontrollable trembles, something she'd never felt before. Her body wouldn't quiet down. "Am I going to be okay?"

They laughed and held her tight.

"Yes, baby." Bane sat up and put on a condom. "We'll make sure you're okay." He crawled up her body.

She could feel his hard cock pressing against her pussy. "I can't believe this. It's so incredible."

"Yes, it is, sweetheart." Adam kissed her shoulder.

"But it's amazing. Don't you understand?"

They laughed again.

"We do, honey." Bane smiled.

Suddenly, the pressure returned, but now it was twice the intensity as before. "Oh my God."

"What? Are you okay?"

"I know this might sound crazy, but I'm feeling things that are completely new to me. Can we do this again? Right now?"

Bane nodded. "Before this night is over, we're going to pleasure you over and over, darlin'. You're going to experience things that will blow your mind. I've got to get inside your gorgeous body. I need to feel your pussy on my dick."

Adam rolled a condom down his shaft. "And I must send my cock into your pretty, sweet ass."

Their lusty words were like gasoline on the fire already burning inside her. "Can we start now?"

"Yes, baby, this is all about you," Adam ran his hand down her body and stopped just above her pussy.

"You're starting the tingles to come again."

"That's what we intend to do. Just let your body go and enjoy each and every touch." Bane continued to gently caress her.

While Bane kissed her breasts softly, Adam lowered his hand on her pussy and very slowly began massaging her.

She felt so relaxed, yet at the same time those wonderful sensations were returning. Adam spread the folds of her pussy and placed his fingers deep inside her.

"You're so wet, sweetheart. Absolutely perfect." He took his fingers out of her pussy and began using her juices to lubricate her ass.

Bane got on his back and rolled her on top of him.

She could feel his massive cock next to her pussy. "Please, Bane, I want you inside me."

"My pleasure, baby." He drove his dick deep inside her to a place she'd never felt before.

"Oh. My. God. I think you hit my G-spot."

Adam got on top of her back and teased her ass with his giant cock.

"Adam I need you to….is it possible for you…to—"

"Yes, I'm going to enter you now, just relax, and I'll go very slow." He pushed his dick past her tight ring and into her ass.

There was a split second of a hot sting as he stretched her in a place she'd never been stretched before. As he and Bane sent their cocks deeper inside her, desire swamped all her nerve endings. "Oh my God. This feels so good. It's electrifying."

They thrust in and out of her.

"It's shivering and crazy and wonderful."

In and out. Over and over.

Everything in her came alive. "I've never thought…God…it's overwhelming."

"Ride it out, sweetheart." Bane's tone deepened.

Adam whispered in her ear, "Tighten your gorgeous body on our cocks. Squeeze down on them. Feel all of us."

Bane reached down and pressed on her throbbing clit.

She screamed and her body seemed to have a mind of its own, writhing between the two men that had given her a second orgasm, this one more intense and powerful than the one before.

Bane and Adam increased their thrusts, slamming into her with abandon. They came together, each groaning her name like a prayer. "Em. Oh, Em. Yes."

She was completely and utterly spent, and yet her body continued to vibrate wildly. "I had no idea it could be like this." Her words came out breathy and so very shaky. Being still or quiet was impossible. "Thank you. My God. I–I can't believe how great I feel. I just love sex. I love it so much."

They laughed and held her tight.

She smiled. "I love it so much with you."

"Baby, you're one in a million." Bane pressed his mouth softly to hers.

"One in a billion, bro." Adam kissed the back of her neck.

Her heart was opening up to them. As she fell asleep in their arms, she realized life had never been better.

Her cell rang.

"Oh God. Not again." The sunrays were coming through the blinds on the window. *It's morning.* She sat up, all her muscles tensing.

"What's the matter?"

She didn't answer, but reached over Bane to grab her phone off the nightstand. When she saw that the call was from Autumn, her shoulders relaxed. "Nothing is the matter. It's one of my girls." She held her index finger to her lips, asking them to be silent.

They nodded.

"Hey, sweetheart."

"Hi, Mom. Have you found a place yet?"

"Yes, honey. Everything is going well. I have a job and a new place."

"What kind of job did you get?" Autumn's curiosity always made her smile.

"I'll tell you all about it when I get back to Grandma and Grandpa's house?"

"When are you coming, Mom? I miss you so much."

"I miss you, too, sweetheart. I will be coming back shortly to pick up our things to move into our new house. And as soon as school is out, I will return and get you and Andrea." That was only a month away, thank God. Any more, and she would've transferred them to Wilde's middle school. She hated being away from them, but she knew it was for the best in the short term.

"I have a concert this weekend. Will you be here for that?"

"Yes, honey. I wouldn't miss it for anything."

"Oh good, Mom. I can't wait to see you and I can't wait to move to Wilde."

"You are going to love our new place. You and Andrea will each get your own room."

"Really? My own room?"

She grinned. "Yes. Your own room."

"Can I decorate it myself?"

She wondered what wild color she would like. "Yes. Let me talk to Andrea."

"She's shopping with Grandma. Larry is here."

The tone in Autumn's voice changed when she mentioned her dad's name. Emma didn't find that strange at all, since her daughter didn't really know him. What she did find odd was how much time Larry was spending with the girls. He'd never shown much interest in them before. She'd seen him disappoint them so often by breaking so many promises and not showing up when he had said he would. *He better not break their hearts again.*

"Larry wants to know the address to our new house, Mom. Do you want to talk to him?"

She sighed, looking at the two wonderful men in her bed. "No, baby. Grab a pen and I'll give you the address to share with him and Grandma."

"I've got one right here."

She gave Autumn the address to the rental house. "I will call you when I'm ready to leave."

"I love you, Mom."

"I love you, too." After the call ended, she turned to Bane and Adam.

"You look happy, Em." Bane cupped her chin.

"I'm very happy to hear from Autumn."

"I'm glad it was one of your daughters instead of whoever you were afraid was calling." Adam was getting too close to the truth.

"What do you mean?"

One of Adam's eyebrows shot up. "We saw how you reacted when your cell rang."

Emma wasn't ready to tell them about the voices. She might not ever be ready to tell anyone. She didn't like to lie, but she didn't have any choice right now. "I thought it was this old friend of mine that just talks and talks and talks. I certainly wasn't in the mood for that. You can understand that, can't you?"

Bane leaned forward. "Sure, sweetheart."

"When are you going back to get your things, Em?" Adam asked.

"I need to clear it with Mac. As you know, she is my new boss. I'm hoping to leave tomorrow, but I need her okay."

He nodded. "We'll help you move your stuff."

"We can rent a truck here and drive down together." Bane traced her bare shoulder with his fingers. "We can make a nice trip out of it."

"Guys, it's over sixteen hours to drive there. That's asking too much of you."

"We're not scheduled to start our new jobs for another week, Em."

Adam smiled. "And if Mac decides you have to wait, it will be easy to get leave."

"You mean time off, bro," Bane said. "We're civilians now."

"Right. Em, we know our supervisor quite well. We served with Caleb during several of our tours."

"Adam and I want to help you. Let us. It would be so much fun for all of us to go together."

"Oh it's really fun when you're loading furniture on a truck," she teased. "I think it would be fun, but I don't want to take advantage of you."

"I don't think you're taking advantage, sweetheart." Adam traced her chin with his finger. "We're the ones who are offering to help you. I, for one, am not ready to be away from you, Em."

"I for two," Bane added.

She smiled. "I for three. Okay. You can help me."

Adam smiled. "Now you're talking, baby."

"Our first road trip together." Bane kissed her. "I've never been to North Dakota before. Maybe we can take a detour and see Mount Rushmore."

She laughed. "That's in South Dakota, soldier. That would be quite the detour."

He shrugged. "Maybe we can plan for it when we go back to get your girls."

"That's a great idea, bro. I can't wait to meet your daughters." Adam kissed her.

She'd been on her own for so long, but now these two amazing men wanted to be there for her. Things were moving quite fast. Too fast. But she couldn't see any reason why she needed to slow things down. Not yet, anyway.

They squeezed her tight between them and she felt her body warm again.

As they showered her with caresses and kisses, she whispered, "Thank you."

It would be wonderful to be able to spend more time with Bane and Adam. Already just being near them had made her feel safe—*and sane.*

Chapter Seven

Emma followed Mac into her new luxurious, gorgeously decorated office. There was a giant desk and credenza, a sitting area with a sofa and chairs, floor-to-ceiling bookshelves, and windows with a gorgeous view. "I can't believe this is going to be mine."

Mac smiled. "But it is yours. The new owners spare no expense, Em."

"But it's so large. You could fit at least two or three more people in here."

"Believe me, you will be using every square inch of it in your new job." Mac pointed to the chair behind the desk. "Try it out."

"You're the boss." She grinned and walked around the desk. She pulled out the chair and took a seat. It was perfectly adjusted for her. "This is unbelievable. Thank you so much for hiring me. I won't let you down."

"I know you won't." Mac sat in one of the two chairs facing her desk. "Let's get down to business. I want you to learn every facet of the television station."

I wonder why.

"I can see you have questions. I'm going to tell you a secret that you cannot tell anyone."

"You can trust me, Mac."

"I'm going to have a baby."

"Oh my God. That's really good news. Congratulations. You will make such a perfect mom."

"Thank you. That's the reason I've got to teach you everything. I will be taking a leave when the baby comes. The newspaper staff can handle it without me, but I need you to hold the reins here at KINK until I return."

"Honestly, I'm overwhelmed. This is my first time in broadcasting."

"Believe me, Em. You will be ready by the time I go in to have my baby."

"When are you due?"

"January next year. I'm only a month along. Wyatt and Wade are so excited. We're going to announce to our friends and family at our summer barbeque on the ranch in June. You will be there, won't you?"

"I would love to." Wilde folks sure did love their events, and there wasn't a better party than hearing someone had gotten engaged or was going to have a baby. She hated to ask for time off since she just got started, but she had no other choice. "I have another question. I need to pack up my apartment and move into my new house. When is a good time for me to take off?"

"North Dakota is a long way from Nevada. Let's make your official start date a week from today. Will that give you enough time?"

"That's more than enough." She looked across her desk at her new boss, who was fast becoming a good friend, too. "I'm sure I can get everything done by then. Thank you so much. Takes a big load off of my mind."

"Do you need any help? My guys could go with you and bring a couple of our ranch hands to help you move the big stuff."

She shook her head. "I've got help. Bane and Adam have agreed to go with me and lend a hand."

"Oh. I see." Mac smiled broadly. "Not just hands. Muscles, too, right? Not to mention their good looks."

"You're right about their good looks and muscles." She grinned. "I guess we'll just have to see about the rest of it."

* * * *

Sitting at his parents' table with Bane, Adam's cell rang with the Marine's Hymn. *From the Halls of Montezuma/ To the shores of Tripoli...*

He looked at his screen and saw the caller was Em. "Hey, sweetheart."

"Got the okay from Mac." Emma sounded happy and relieved. "She gave me a week to get everything done. How soon can you and Bane be ready?"

"We are ready." He held up his thumb to Bane, letting him know things were on target. "Just been waiting for your phone call."

She laughed, which was a sound he was certain he would never tire of. "I need a little more time, Adam. Can you give me an hour?"

"You got it, Em. We'll be at the hotel with the truck to pick you up."

"You already got a truck, too?"

"We're Marines. We're always prepared."

"I can see that. Okay. I'll see you shortly. Thank you so much for this."

"It's our pleasure, sweetheart." When the call ended, he turned to Bane. "Just like we thought. Wyatt and Wade's wife gave Em all the time she needed. We leave in an hour."

"Good thing we already packed." Their suitcases were by the front door.

"It wasn't hard, bro. We've only been back in town a couple of days, and we haven't completely unpacked yet." He and Bane were set up in Carolyn's old room for the time being. Carolyn hadn't returned, but had finally called to check on Shelby and the baby. The whole family still held hope for Carolyn to find happiness one day.

"We need to let Mom and Dads know that it's a sure thing we're leaving." Their parents were over at Shelby's with the baby. "I doubt they will even notice we're gone."

"You got that right." Bane smiled. "Who can blame them, bro? Grace Madelyn is the prettiest little angel I've ever seen. That pink

Teddy bear we got her is bigger than she is."

They both laughed.

"Yes, she is. Our niece looks so much like, Sis." Adam was thrilled to be an uncle. He wanted to have his own children one day, too. He and Bane, having grown up in Wilde, would build a family together. *Em?* "What did you think about Em's reaction to the phone call she got this morning?"

Bane shook his head. "She actually looked frightened to me."

"I thought so, too. I don't buy what she told us. Do you?"

"Not a single word of it. Something shook her pretty hard. Maybe we can get her to open up to us on the trip. A little BDSM play might do the trick."

"Bro, she's been away from Wilde a very long time. She left when she was a teenager." Still he would love to see how she responded to two Doms. He had a hunch she would love to be dominated. "I doubt she's been exposed to the life."

"You're probably right, but I find her so desirable. I know it's early, but I believe she's the one." Bane's confession was something new. Em had impacted his brother as much as him. "Do you feel the same, Adam?"

"We're twins, bro. Of course I do. I'm nuts for her already. I can't get her out of my mind."

Bane nodded. "I think it's time to move things further along with her."

"I completely agree."

* * * *

"Sir, is this your bag?"

Larry put on his best smile for the TSA agent. "Yes, it is." As he'd expected, the equipment inside was causing him some grief.

"Please stand there. I'm going to inspect your luggage. Do not touch or reach into your bag while I'm conducting the inspection. Are there any items you need to declare before I begin?"

Larry handed the agent the paperwork he'd forged from his company. "This is a list of the items that are inside. You'll find remote access security surveillance equipment."

The agent looked at the list and handed it back to him. "Thank you."

Larry watched her unzip the bag with her gloved hands. It was obvious by the agent's demeanor she had no clue she was looking at the latest technology on the market. The cables, cameras, DVR, and speakers could be used in several ways besides what they'd been intended for by the manufacturer, especially after being modified.

Chapter Eight

"It's twenty-one hundred. I think it's time to find a decent place to stay for the night." Bane kept his hands on the steering wheel. "We're just five miles from Casper."

"It's a good halfway point." Emma stretched her arms. "Right when you get inside the city limits there's a hotel I've stayed at whenever I went to visit Mom." She sighed. "I miss her, you know."

Adam placed his hand on her knee. "Norma was a wonderful woman, Em."

"Yes, she was." She put on a brave face. God, Bane couldn't get over how strong she was. Em had suffered so much, losing her mother to her crazy homicidal sister, and still, she found a way through the pain. "Anyway, the rooms are lovely and clean. Plus, the hotel has a great breakfast buffet. Biscuits and gravy. Yum."

"Sounds like a plan to me." Bane drove into town and pulled into the parking lot of the hotel Em had recommended.

"I'll go get the room." Adam jumped out of the cab.

He nodded. "Em and I will stay by the truck until you get back. That'll give us time to stretch our legs."

After Adam left, Bane helped Emma out of the cab. "I thought he'd never leave."

"Why?"

He smiled. "Come here, you." He put his arms around her. Holding her close, he leaned in and pressed his lips to hers. He traced his tongue over her lips. God, she was utter feminine perfection. "I've been wanting to do that ever since we left Wilde."

She smiled. "Was it worth waiting for, soldier?"

"If I had to wait a hundred years knowing I would just get one more kiss from you, it would be worth the wait."

"It was pretty damn good, wasn't it?" She laughed and looked up at him. "Thank you again for doing this for me. It's going to be quite the job when we get to my apartment. I haven't packed a single box. I had no idea things were going to work out so fast in Wilde."

"I'm glad they did, baby." He held her quietly for several minutes.

"Where is Adam? It never took me this long to get registered at this hotel."

"I'm not sure." The parking lot was almost empty, which was a sure sign the place had a ton of vacancies. "But does it matter? It gives me more time to kiss those beautiful lips of yours."

"I think Adam deserves a kiss, too. Don't you agree?"

He grinned. "Adam can fight his own battles. I'm sure he'll steal some kisses from you whenever he gets the chance, but for now, he's not here. We are."

"I thought you wanted us to stretch our legs, not our lips."

"Lips or legs? Does it really matter? I like both on you, sweetheart."

"You're a devil, Bane, aren't you?"

He thought about what he and Adam had planned for the evening. "I guess I am." He bent down and devoured her lips, relishing the sweetness he tasted there.

"What's going on, you two?" Adam smiled with the card key to their room in his hand. "I leave for a few minutes and come back catching you two kissing. Fair is fair. It's my turn."

Bane nodded as his brother pulled Emma into his chest and planted a lip-lock on her that seemed to take her breath away.

"Now," Adam said. "That's better."

Bane laughed. "I'm still one up on you, bro."

"Not for long. The night is young."

Em shook her head. "You two are trouble with a capital *T*."

"You bet we are, baby." Adam put his arm around her. "Number

222 is on the second floor. We can park around back. There's an entrance there and we can go up the stairs to our room. The lady at the desk said it was the first door on the left."

After the short drive to the parking area, they climbed out of the car and walked up the stairs and into their room.

"Wow, this is a big sized room." Em walked over to the table, which had a bottle of wine on it. "Mine was never this big and I never got one of these." She pointed to the bottle.

Adam grinned. "Perhaps they are going upscale since you were here last, baby."

He and Adam placed the bags on the bed.

"I sure could use a shower," Adam said. "How about you two?"

"You've got that right, bro."

"How do we choose who goes first?" Em asked. "Rock, paper, scissors?"

"We don't have to choose. Let's shower together." Adam grabbed the bag with the handcuffs, blindfold, and headphones they'd brought.

Bane was in complete sync with his brother. There was no time like the present to get to the night's activities they'd planned for Emma.

"You two are big Marines. I don't think we could all fit. The room might be bigger but the bathroom is likely the same size as the other rooms here."

"Yes, we can fit." Adam winked. "I got a handicap room so we could clean up together, baby."

Emma looked around. "What if someone really needs this room?"

"According to the lady, they have nine more rooms just like this one and all of them are vacant. I don't think it will be a problem." Adam walked over to the bathroom door and swung it open. "So let's just enjoy ourselves."

She nodded.

The bathroom was huge with a shower to die for. It had a rain showerhead, six square body sprays, and one handheld wand. There were luxurious shampoos, soaps, and sponges.

"Candles?" Emma turned to Adam. "Now I know you had something to do with this, didn't you? That's why it took you so long to get the room."

"Yes, I did."

Bane appreciated his brother's finesse. "Way to go, bro. I couldn't be more proud of you."

"I set this all up with Hazel. She's a doll and a complete romantic." Adam pulled Emma into another kiss and slowly removed her top.

"Looks like she's not the only romantic around here." Bane kissed the back of Emma's neck, letting his hands drift down her arms.

God, I love how soft her skin is to the touch.

While Adam gently removed the rest of Emma's clothes, Bane went into the bathroom and turned on the shower. He wanted to make sure it was the perfect temperature for her. He removed his clothes, and then tested the water. It felt just right. Nice and warm.

He turned around and saw Adam had taken off his clothing, too. "The shower is ready for us."

Adam nodded. "Now that we're all completely naked, it's time to start our shower with this beautiful woman." His brother lifted Emma into his arms and carried her to the warm water. Adam put her down very carefully, making sure she wouldn't slip.

As the warm water drifted down her skin, Bane just wanted to look at her and take in her beauty. "You are so fucking gorgeous, Emma. Have I ever told you that before?"

"Yes, you have, many times, but now I realize you actually mean it. It's not just a line."

"Let me show you how much I mean it." He pressed his mouth on hers and kissed her deeply, with such passion, he felt her legs begin to wobble. The little moans that came from her made Bane want her even more. His cock was hard as a rock and his balls were so heavy.

Adam held her from behind and steadied her. "I need to kiss those sweet lips too, bro."

"Yes, you do. Let me turn her for you." Bane moved Emma around until she was facing Adam.

His brother placed his mouth on hers.

Bane could see, like him, his brother's cock was fully erect. It was evident that Adam wanted Emma to know how much he desired her. They both stood under the rain showerhead as they continued kissing.

Adam began washing her front with his soapy hands.

Bane grabbed the shampoo bottle and squeezed out some of its contents into his palm. He threaded his fingers through her red, silky locks. Deep thundering longing pounded inside him.

"Okay, let's rinse your hair now, baby."

She leaned her head back until her hair was completely soaked. He slowly and meticulously worked all the shampoo out of her hair. Adam continued cleaning her with his fingers, spending a great deal of time on her breasts.

After rinsing her hair, Bane soaped down her back with his hands, loving the feel of her. He burned. The need to be inside her hot little body was driving him mad.

He reached down and cleaned her gorgeous ass. "Does this feel good, sweetheart?"

"Yes. Oh yes. It feels amazing."

He ran his hand between her ass cheeks and began fingering her anus.

He felt her squeeze her thighs together. She was clearly on fire. *Perfect. Just like we want you, sweetheart. Lost to your passion.*

Adam knelt down in front of her. "God, this is the most beautiful pussy in the world."

Emma shook her head. "Pussies aren't beautiful."

"Yours is, baby." His brother's tone deepened. "Yours is a work of art."

Adam's words had a visible impact on her, and Bane could feel her little trembles as he moved his hands around her to her breasts.

"Come on, guys. Nothing about me is a work of art, but I do like my hair."

"So you think Adam is a liar." He used his most forceful tone, desiring a submissive response from her. "Because if you do, then you think I'm a liar, too."

"I–I don't understand."

Bane could tell she was burning with want but at the same time her self-doubt was trying to reemerge and take her over. "Let me make it very clear to you, then." He stopped touching her, pulling his hands off her soft body. It was the last thing he wanted to do, but he knew it was what he must do to move things the direction he and Adam had planned for her. Though he couldn't see Adam clearly, he was certain he'd stopped touching her, too. They were always in sync when it came to pleasuring and dominating a woman. "You are the most beautiful creature I've ever laid eyes on. Adam thinks so, too. So are you going to call us both liars?"

"No. I would never do that. I'm sorry. Really, I am."

Jackpot. You're ours now, little sub. "Then trust us when we say you are beautiful."

"I want to, but I just don't see myself that way."

"You will by the time this night is over, sweetheart," Adam said. "Say it, Em. Tell us you are beautiful."

"I can't."

Bane licked her neck and swirled his thumbs over her taut nipples. "So you do think we are liars. Not good, baby. Not good at all." He pinched her sweet little nubs, clamping down on her earlobe with his teeth at the same time.

"Oh God. Damn. So good." She panted, stoking his heat even more.

He whispered in her ear. "Baby, we want to pleasure you, but you have to earn it."

"Please. I can't stand much more. I need you so badly."

"I'm not sure we believe you." Adam clearly was enjoying her suffering. "I want to taste and touch your tight, pretty pussy, but I'm not sure I should since you think we are just feeding you lines about your looks."

"No. I–I believe you. I do. Please. I'll do anything to prove it to you."

Bane kissed the back of her neck, enjoying the tremble it incited from her. "Anything?"

"Yes. I swear. Just please don't stop touching me."

That's what we've been waiting for. "You're going to have to prove it to us."

"Yes. I will. What do I need to do to make you believe me?"

Adam laughed. "Listen to her. This little thing didn't believe us at first and now she wants us to believe her."

"I swear I'm telling the truth."

Bane turned off the shower and began caressing her once again, paying special attention to her breasts with one hand and moving the other down her body to her pussy.

Adam stepped out of the shower to the bag he'd set on the countertop. His brother pulled out the blindfold. "Trust is an important thing to Bane and I. Are you willing to wear this for us as an act of trust, sweetheart?"

"Yes. Anything. I swear."

God, she is so perfect in every way. "What do you know about BDSM, baby?"

"I know some. I am originally from Wilde, though I've never been to The Masters' Chambers."

That was the BDSM club just outside of town. "Tell us what you know."

"You should have a safe word. I remember that."

"Very good. I promise that you won't be disappointed. How about Adam and I help you dip your toe in the BDSM waters, baby?"

Chapter Nine

"Yes. Please." Emma had hoped there would be some lovemaking tonight with Bane and Adam, but she had never dreamed they would introduce her to something she'd fantasized about again and again. "Tell me what to do, Bane. I want to experience BDSM with you and Adam."

They both smiled broadly.

As they dried her off with the plush towels, Bane began giving her instructions. "Our lifestyle is about trust that is reached between Doms and their subs through protocols. It can be a very structured kind of sexual discovery."

"I've had very little personal discovery in my life, guys, though I've read a ton on the subject."

"Reading is good, honey, but experiencing is a whole other ball game."

"You said you knew about safe words. Let's settle on one for tonight's play, baby," Adam said. "This is how it works…"

As they continued telling her about BDSM, heat ran up and down her body from all the attention they were giving her. They'd made her feel special and beautiful with every touch and kiss, something she'd never received before.

Long ago she'd come up with the word she wanted to use if she ever got this kind of opportunity. "Would 'pancake' be okay for the safe word for tonight?"

They grinned.

"Why 'pancake'?" Bane asked.

"Because I always eat too many and I have to stop."

"You've picked a great word, darlin'." Adam's hot gaze made her tremble. "Time for your first lesson."

Her excitement overtook her, and she jumped up into his arms, wrapping her legs around his waist and her arms around his neck. "That wasn't very submissive of me, was it?"

Adam held her tight. "You're quite eager, aren't you?"

"Yes. This is a dream come true."

"Damn, you're a dream for us, sweetheart." Bane led them into the other room. "We are in play, now. You are the submissive and we are the Doms. Do you understand?"

She nodded.

Adam lowered her to the mattress. "Were you listening when we were telling you the protocols, sub?" His tone had a sexy edge to it.

"I was. I promise." It was clear she was doing something wrong, but what?

He and Bane shook their heads. They were identical in both looks and how they acted.

"Tell us the truth, sub." Bane cupped her chin. "You were only half listening, correct?"

Oh my God. I forgot how I'm supposed to address them. She lowered her eyes. "Yes, Master."

He grinned. "Very good."

"I tried to pay complete attention to you and Master Adam, but my mind was wandering. I was so excited."

"We're going to test you, sub." Adam placed the blindfold over her eyes.

Losing sight had the strangest impact on her, but she certainly wasn't going to say "pancake." Without the ability to use her eyes, her other senses seemed to sharpen. Bane and Adam ran their fingers up and down her body freely as they'd done before, but this time, without sight, her skin seemed to respond even more. Every inch of her was tingling.

"Sirs, I just love this. It's amazing."

"If that's amazing, how does this make you feel, sub?" Bane pinched her nipples, delivering a sharp, sweet sting that sent an electric shock down to her pussy.

"Incredible, Boss…I mean, Sir…Master. Oh God. I'm so sorry for messing up, but this is overwhelming. May we please do more?"

He brushed his mouth over hers, and she tasted him on her lips. "You're not messing up at all, baby. You're doing perfect. And yes, we will do more."

"You are the best Doms in all the world." When they didn't respond, she wondered if she'd made a mistake. "Should I have said that, Sirs?"

They both laughed.

"You keep saying whatever comes into that pretty little head of yours, honey." Bane's words were deeper than she'd ever heard them before. They had a rumble to them that vibrated along her skin. "You're doing everything right."

"Damn, woman. You're perfect." Adam's tone was full of lust. His lips feathered her ear, and she inhaled his manly scent. "You're making it difficult for me to control myself, and I've been in the life for years. I've never come across anyone so wonderful as you."

"Let's turn the heat up on this precious sub, bro."

She wondered what Bane meant by that, but didn't have to wait long to find out. He pulled her arms over her head and attached what she knew had to be handcuffs on her wrists. Now she was without sight and couldn't move her arms. Her heart thudded in her chest as their dominance continued to raise her temperature. She trusted them fully, but it was still a little unnerving—*but oh so worth it.*

Bane and Adam's soft touches turned to little kisses on her neck and pinches on her nipples, making her body squirm and her clit throb. "Yes, Sirs. Yes. So good."

"Keep talking, sub," Bane said. "Tell us how you're feeling."

"Yes, Masters. I feel everything. This is beyond good." A pressure grew inside her, pushing her need higher and higher. "I never knew it could be so damn wonderful. There has got to be at least a hundred thousand nerve endings inside me that have been dormant my whole life. Not anymore. Not after tonight. Not after being with you."

"We're about to turn on another million nerve endings in you, baby." Bane touched her pussy, causing her toes to curl and her core to swirl with want. "Nice and wet. Perfect."

He rolled her onto his lap. She could feel his hard cock pressing into her belly. Not the place she needed it to be. *Maybe if I move just right, I can get it to a better position, touching my pussy.*

"I'm going to spank you for not believing us when we said you were beautiful."

"Sir, I believe you. I really do." Excitement and nervousness danced together inside her, tugging and pulling each other in her mind.

"But you don't believe it yourself. You still don't see what we see. Hell, you don't see what the entire world sees. That's why we're going to spank this gorgeous ass of yours. Do you understand that you need to be punished?"

"Yes, Sir, but I'm a little nervous."

"Do you trust us?" Adam's tone made her tremble.

"Yes. I trust you, Masters."

"I'm going to give you five slaps, sub." Bane's hands cupped her ass. "You will count them out aloud. Every one of them. Understand?"

"Yes, Sir." She curled her fingers, making fists of her hands, readying herself for the onslaught to come.

Bane's hand landed on her ass with an audible smack.

"One, Sir." The burn spread from where he'd hit her bottom throughout the rest of her body. Her swollen lips and nipples got a dose of the energy, but most of the transferred heat landed between her legs, causing her pussy to clench.

"Baby, you're doing great," Adam whispered in her ear. "Let me help you get through this." She felt him reach under her and thread his fingers through her swollen folds.

"God, yes." When he circled her clit with his thumb, her erotic pressure shot up threefold.

Another smack from the sexy Marine Dom made her eyes water. "Two, Sir."

What had been hot before inside her now seemed to be even stronger, almost to the boiling point.

Smack.

"Three, Sir."

Their treatment of her, Adam fingering her pussy and Bane spanking her ass, took her almost to the edge.

"Two more, sub." Bane ran his finger between her legs, touching her anus. "Just two more."

"Yes, Sir. I can take it."

"I know you can, baby. You're gorgeous, smart, and unbelievably incredible."

His praise made her feel so good. If he and Bane saw her that way, why couldn't it be true? She was beginning to see herself differently, to see herself through their eyes. *Maybe I am beautiful.*

"Ready?"

"Yes, Sir. I'm ready."

He landed the next two slaps to her ass back to back, one right after another.

"Four. Five, Sir." Even though she was still in the blindfold, she closed her eyes, trying to ride out the smoldering of her bottom.

Bane reached down and kissed the spots he'd spanked. Feeling his lips on her ass, which was already burning like lava, made her even hotter.

When he licked her anus, she writhed with want. "Please, Masters. Please. I need you inside me so badly."

"Keep up the begging, sub." Bane's volume softened, though his words remained full of dominance. "We love to hear it, but we are the ones who decide when you get your reward."

"My turn to spank this ass." Adam patted her bottom. "But before I do, I'm going to remove the blindfold and handcuffs."

Bane handed her over to Adam, placing her on his lap. They took off her restraints and blindfold.

She blinked several times as her focus returned.

"See this?" Adam held up a large paddle in front of her eyes. It was black with holes bored into its surface.

"Yes, Sir," she choked out, a little terrified by the thing.

"This is what I'm going to spank you with, sub. Five times. Five slaps to your ass. You. Are. Beautiful. Instead of counting out a number, I want you to say out loud 'I am beautiful.' Understand me?"

"Yes, Master."

"Look at me, sub."

She turned her head and looked up at him.

"I want to make sure you do understand. Tell me what you are going to say when this beast bites your ass?"

"I–I am b–beautiful, Sir."

He smiled. "That's right. Head down. We are about to begin."

She lowered her gaze, bracing herself for what was to come. Her breathing was shallow and her heartbeats were fast. She waited for the first chomp of the paddle.

"God, you are something else, baby." Adam rubbed the flat surface of the beast on her ass. "Can you imagine how this is going to feel on you? It's going to get you to another level of excitement."

She was vibrating wildly, waiting for him to begin. Why was he holding back her punishment?

Her breaths were caught in her chest. She just knew the first smack would come any second. When it didn't, she began to count in her head, trying to calm her nervous anticipation. It didn't work to quell anything, including the pressure that continued to grow and grow inside her. They'd been right. Her books had given her a glimpse into how pain could be so pleasurable but experiencing for herself in her flesh was beyond anything she'd ever imagined. Though the paddle made her tremble, she also desired Adam to kiss her ass with it.

Bane moved his fingers between her legs. When he touched her pussy and clit, Adam finally slapped her ass with the beast.

The mix of pain and pleasure drove her crazy.

"I'm waiting, sub." Adam fingered her anus, sending one of his digits into her ass.

"I am beautiful, Sirs."

"Yes, you are, Em." Adam smacked her ass again with the paddle, its bite even more intense than the first time. And again, he and Bane touched her ass and pussy just right, making her deliciously dizzy.

"I am beautiful, Sirs."

Three more whacks, each followed with the response he'd demanded from her. She felt tears streaming down her cheeks, her ass burning hot, her pussy clenching tight, her clit throbbing violently.

She whispered once again, "I am beautiful." And for the first time in her life, she believed it. "Masters, can this beautiful woman come now? Have I earned my reward?"

"Yes, you can, baby. You've earned this." Adam thrust a couple of fingers into her ass. "Come for us, Em."

Bane pressed on her clit with his thumb and sent his fingers deep inside her pussy.

Their finger fucking sent her over the edge and into much-needed release. The giant ball of pressure exploded into a climatic wave of electricity throughout her body. Shaking with such uncontrollable turbulence, she would've fallen to the floor had Bane and Adam not held her in place. Finally, her body completely relaxed.

She sat up between them on the bed, catching her breath. "That was incredible, Sirs. I feel so connected to you. I really want to do something for you, too." She reached out and grabbed their hard cocks. "May I?"

Adam laughed and Bane smiled.

"Look at this little sub," Adam said. "One night in the life and she's already trying to top us from the bottom."

She got down on the floor between them. "But I did ask, Masters."

Bane grinned. "Yes, you did. Permission granted."

She gave them her best salute. "Thank you, Sirs." Holding both of their thick dicks in her hands, she leaned forward and kissed the tips of their cocks. They both rewarded her with pearly drops of what was to come. She bathed them with her tongue, running it up and down their long, hard shafts one after the other, over and over.

"Damn that feels so good." Adam growled his approval.

Bane threaded his fingers through her hair.

She swallowed Adam's cock while stroking Bane's dick. After a few bobs up and down Adam, she switched positions, sucking on Bane's cock and fisting Adam's. Back and forth between them, she continued pleasuring them with her hands and mouth.

"Enough." Bane tugged on her hair.

"Did I do something wrong, Sir?"

He smiled. "No. You did everything right, sub, but I want to be inside your pretty little ass. That's how I'm going to come tonight."

"And I'm going to send my cock into your tight pussy, baby." Adam donned a condom. "Another time, I'm going to shoot my seed down your thirsty throat, but not tonight."

They lifted her onto the bed. Adam stretched out next to her, helping her on top of his muscled body. She could feel his cock pressing on her clit, which sent a fresh round of shivers through her. From behind, Bane held her legs apart as Adam thrust his cock into her aching pussy. When he hit her G-spot, she moaned. Bane applied lubricant to her ass and climbed on top of her, pinning her between him and Adam. It felt so right to be with them, so perfect.

Bane sent his cock into her ass. They began thrusting into her, stretching her insides and delivering a myriad of sensations throughout her body.

Lost to her pleasure, she writhed between them, enjoying every stroke.

In a unified yell, the three of them came together. Being completely sated and spent, they fell asleep in each other's arms.

Chapter Ten

Emma awoke early the next morning sandwiched in between Bane and Adam.

She sat up slowly, quietly, trying not to disturb the two Doms. Looking at their muscled bodies gave her a slight tingle. They'd given her the most wonderful sex she'd ever experienced in her life and had shown her things she never thought she would ever have the pleasure of enjoying.

Adam opened his eyes and stretched his arms over his head. "Good morning, sweetheart. How did you sleep?"

So much for trying not to disturb them. "Like a log. How about you?"

"Very sound as well. I would like a strong cup of coffee though to get the ol' body going."

"Coming right up. I'll get it started." She headed into the bathroom where the coffeemaker was. "It'll give me a minute to freshen up."

* * * *

Bane opened his eyes and pushed the covers back. "Hey, bro, how long have you been awake?"

"Just now."

"Where's Em?" He swung his legs over the side of the bed.

"She's making coffee." Adam pointed to the closed door.

"Do you know when she wants to leave?"

"Probably after breakfast. We'll have to try the buffet she was talking about."

"That sounds great, I'm absolutely famished after last night."

"Me, too."

Bane got out of bed and turned to Adam. "God, bro, she is so wonderful. She is perfect. She is everything I've dreamed about. I am falling in love with her."

"Me, too, but we don't want to scare her off." Adam was right about that.

Even after the incredible night they had with her, Bane believed she needed a little more time. "Just look at all she's been through, but I still want to talk to her about that phone call. That was the plan, remember?"

Adam nodded. "Maybe she will open up to us now. There's no doubt about her trusting us."

"Let's try at breakfast, if it feels right. If not, we still have a long ride in the truck to bring up the subject."

* * * *

Emma finished brushing her teeth.

She looked in the mirror at her reflection and smiled. "I am beautiful, but this face still needs some makeup."

She laughed, pulling out her base. Applying her makeup as the smell of fresh coffee filled the space, she couldn't remember a time she'd been so happy. The reason? Bane and Adam were the reason, of course.

She'd gotten a little taste of their Dom sides and she wanted a second and third helping. She could tell that they knew so much more about BDSM. It would be amazing to be their student in the lifestyle.

I wish they could be in my life forever.

What are you thinking, Em? Don't forget the voices in your head.

She closed her eyes, feeling the weight of the past year on her shoulders. Remembering how it had all started, she thought about her mother and Lily's funeral. That was when she'd begun hearing her two dead sister's voices at night.

But whenever I'm with Bane and Adam, I don't hear them. It's got to be just stress.

She opened her eyes and looked back at her reflection. "I won't go crazy like Samantha and Lily."

She smiled and poured three cups of coffee, one for her and the other two for Bane and Adam, the men who kept the voices away.

* * * *

Emma watched Adam load up his plate at the breakfast buffet for the third time. "He's got quite the appetite, doesn't he?"

Bane held her hand. "Always has."

"Adam won the pie-eating contest back in high school, didn't he?"

"I'm surprised you remember that, Em. You were only a freshman. Yes, Adam did win." The love for his brother was evident on Bane's face. "All us football players had to eat as many pies as we could to raise money for the team. Actually, if I'm honest, I have about as big an appetite as Adam. I came in a close second."

She laughed. "I knew it. Why don't you go fill your plate again? I can see you want to."

Adam came back with his plate stacked high with pancakes. "I brought some for you, Em." He took a fork and placed half of them on her plate.

"Pancake, Sir. Although I wouldn't mind being naughty again with you."

They laughed.

"We'd love to train you, Em," Bane said.

Adam nodded. "You took to the life like a fish to water last night. You're a natural."

"I love to swim."

They laughed again, and she joined in.

"Seriously, Adam. I couldn't eat another bite."

Bane pulled her plate in front of him. "Okay, sweetheart. I'll take care of these for you."

"Guys, I know I've said it several times, but I am so grateful for all you're doing for me. I'm not sure how I would've been able to make this move on my own."

Adam leaned over and kissed her. She could taste a hint of the syrup on his lips. "Baby, you aren't alone. We are here for you."

"I know. It means the world to me."

"Em, you can trust us." Bane squeezed her hand. "You know that, right?"

"Of course." She squeezed his hand back. "I trust you both completely."

"Good. Tell us why you reacted so strongly to that phone call back in Wilde. Honey, you looked so frightened when your cell rang. Whatever it is that you're dealing with, we're here for you."

She held her breath. This wasn't how she wanted things to go.

"Did it have something to do with your girls?" Adam touched her cheek. "Are you worried about someone hurting them?"

She looked into their eyes, which were filled with concern. "Guys, you're right. There is something going on with me, but I'm not worried about anyone hurting my girls." *Except me if I go completely off the rails.* "I promise I will tell you. I just need a little more time. Please understand."

They both nodded.

Bane kissed her on the cheek. "Sweetheart, you are not alone in whatever you are dealing with. Know that."

"I do." God, everything Bane and Adam did melted her heart. They were so perfect. She loved how caring and kind they were, but she was also drawn to their strength and intensity. *God, I want to tell them. I do. I just need the right time and place.*

"We better get going," Bane said. "We don't want you to be late for Autumn's concert."

Autumn's concert. That's tonight. Should I ask them to go with me?

She hadn't expected to start dating again for some time. In fact, she'd thought about waiting until both her girls were out of high school, which would be in five years.

"Guys, you seem anxious to meet my girls, but I must tell you, in the past I have never allowed Autumn and Andrea to meet anyone I was dating. Their father, my ex, hasn't been in their lives much until recently. They don't really have a relationship with him. It's hard on girls to be without a dad to look up to. I don't want them to get attached to other men in my life and get their hearts broken. I want you to meet them, but I want them to see you as my friends only for now. Will you agree to that?"

Adam nodded. "Of course, sweetheart."

Bane put his arm around her shoulders. "It's clear that Autumn and Andrea have a wonderful mom."

* * * *

"Would you like something to drink?" the flight attendant asked sweetly.

Larry had bedded his share of "air mattresses" over the past several years, but he wasn't about to lower his standards ever, though the airlines had certainly lowered theirs these days. He liked the woman's size but her face was downright ugly. "Scotch, straight up, baby."

She smiled. "That will be six dollars, sir."

He handed her his credit card, which was reaching his spending limit fast. He wasn't worried, knowing the windfall he'd been working on for the past several months was about to pay off.

She handed him his cocktail.

"Thank you. When will we be landing in North Dakota, honey?"

"In a little over an hour." The woman moved down the aisle

taking other passengers' drink orders.

His plan was going off without a hitch. He would be back in time to make Autumn's concert and none would be the wiser he'd been away.

He brought the plastic cup up to his lips and swallowed half its contents. The burn it sent down his throat felt good. Leaning back in the uncomfortable coach seat, he smiled.

From now on, first class all the way.

No one in that backwater town of Nevada had seen him break into Emma's new rent house.

He'd placed the cameras and speakers in the air vents. After a quick check that he could operate them from his laptop, he'd left. He'd driven the rental car back to the motel in Elko to grab a few hours' sleep before heading to the airport for his flight back.

The bitch thought she could get away from the voices, but she was wrong.

He smiled.

Hiring that fucking slut at the bar who could imitate celebrities had been a cakewalk. The cunt was desperate for money and affection, playing right into his hands. It had taken the woman less than a week of studying the videos he'd borrowed from Emma and her grandparents to sound exactly like Lily and Samantha. Once this whole thing was over, he would kick the mimic bitch out of his bed for good.

God, it was so good to know that all his hard work was about to reward him with millions.

Once he got Emma committed for insanity, he would get custody of their two snot-nosed girls. Playing loving daddy made him sick to his stomach, but he would only have to keep up the charade for just a little longer. Autumn and Andrea would be sent away to boarding school once he had control of their grandparents' land, which was worth so much more than any of them had a clue.

Working as a geologist for the oil and gas industry, he'd been in the know about the tests his company had conducted in the area around Helen and Leland's land. Several months ago, he'd snuck onto their property and conducted his own tests. His analysis was conclusive. Emma's grandparents' farm was in the very heart of the biggest oil reserves in the entire state. The top oil companies would soon be trying to snatch up control of the oil by offering lucrative leases to landowners. He had a couple of months, maybe less, to finish his plan. He estimated that Helen and Leland's lease offer would net two to ten million over the next five years. He would be set for life.

Those old fools were still on their guard with him, but that wouldn't matter once Emma was out of the picture. No one would suspect a thing. Being a geologist, it would be easy for him to make it look like the two ancient fucks died in their sleep. *Carbon monoxide.*

The flight attendant returned, smiling broadly. "Would you like another? On me."

He grabbed the ugly bitch's hand. "Why not?"

Chapter Eleven

Emma walked into her girls' middle school's auditorium with Bane and Adam. The stage was filled with seats for the student musicians and a grand piano filled the center of the platform, which she found odd.

She scanned the seats and saw Andrea sitting with her grandparents four rows back from the stage.

"There they are." She pointed to her loved ones. "Remember, we're just friends."

"Just friends." Bane nodded. "Got it."

Adam winked.

She knew they were more than friends after all the time they'd spent with each other, but was glad Adam and Bane were willing to keep that quiet for now.

They headed down the aisle.

"Mom, you made it." Andrea jumped up and hugged her.

"Of course I made it, sweetheart. I wouldn't have missed this for the world."

"Autumn is going to be so happy," her grandmother said. "We saved three seats for you and your friends."

Emma had called ahead, telling her grandmother that she was bringing Bane and Adam to the concert.

Bane held out his hand. "Mr. Harris, Mrs. Harris, nice to meet you. I'm Bane Taylor."

Her grandfather shook his hand. "Nice to meet you, too. Am I seeing double, Mr. Taylor?"

Bane grinned. "No sir. This is my twin brother Adam."

Adam shook hands with her grandfather and kissed her grandmother on the cheek.

"Thank God. I thought Helen was going to have to take me to the eye doctor to get my glasses checked."

"Leland, hush up." Her grandmother smiled. "Thank you for helping Emma with her move. It's good to know she has such nice friends."

Adam turned to her daughter. "And you must be Andrea."

"I am. Pleased to meet both of you."

She was proud of how polite Andrea was being.

"And your mother told us that you play the piano quite well," Bane said.

Andrea shrugged, but the smile on her face could not be missed. "My sister and I play duets for our grandparents and their friends."

"Don't be modest, child. Our granddaughters play for all kinds of events around town," her grandfather said with pride. "They will be missed. Our girls are very talented, gentlemen."

Emma knew that her girls were exceptionally gifted.

Adam grinned. "Would you play for us, Andrea?"

Smiling, her daughter nodded. "Mom, you sit next to Grandma and I'll sit with Bane and Adam. Okay?"

"Sure, sweetheart." Emma was shocked to see how quickly Andrea was warming up to Adam and Bane.

They all took their seats. Andrea continued talking to Bane and Adam about music, her favorite topic.

Emma's grandfather sat on the other side of her grandmother. "Honey, if you and your friends need any help packing up your apartment, let us know."

"I will, Grandpa. Thank you for offering"

He winked and sat back in his chair.

Emma turned to her grandmother and said softly, "Thank you so much for everything, Grandma."

"Sweetheart, your girls are no trouble at all." Her grandmother leaned forward and looked past her to Bane and Adam. When her blue-eyed gaze returned to Emma, her lips curled up into a smile. "Just friends?"

"Grandma, please." She'd never been able to hide anything from her grandmother.

"Just saying, dear. My eyes still work well, and I notice how you look at each other."

"You always could read me well, Grandma. I am quite fond of them, but I don't want to let on to the girls just yet. Don't know where this is going and I don't want them hurt."

Her grandmother placed her hand over hers. "Of course you don't, angel. You are such a good mother."

"I don't know about that, but I do try. By the way, where is Larry?"

Her grandmother frowned. "You know him. He probably won't even show up."

She sighed. "I thought he might start coming around more. He seemed different that day he came up on your porch. My girls could use more attention from him."

"Mark my words, Emma. He's up to something. I don't trust him. The one thing I'm glad about you moving to Wilde is, Larry will likely never see Autumn and Andrea again."

"Grandma, he has visitation rights. It's in the court order."

"And how many times has he visited them since they were born." Her grandmother held up her hand. "I bet I have enough fingers to count his visits. It's strange to me that all of a sudden he's Mr. Nice Guy, Mr. Dad. He's up to something."

"Maybe." She couldn't deny her grandmother's logic. Larry always did have a scheme going.

"Autumn and Andrea are so uncomfortable when Larry comes around now." Her grandmother shook her head. "I try to make his visits as short as possible. He keeps bringing gifts for them and for Leland and I. Something doesn't smell right about it at all to me. Your girls don't even know him, Emma. It's best it stays that way."

If she hadn't started hearing her dead sister's voices, she would've thought so, too. In her heart she hoped he would come around. Her grandparents might need his help raising the girls if she lost her mind completely.

Stop it, Emma. I am not going to lose my mind.

Her grandmother touched her arm. "Emma, look how Andrea is smiling at those two. I've never seen her come out of her shell so fast before, have you?"

She turned and saw Andrea more animated than she'd seen her in a very long time. "Bane and Adam are good men."

"I'm sure they are, sweetheart." Her grandmother patted her hand.

The conductor and the students took the stage.

Emma waved at Autumn. Her daughter smiled back.

"Parents and friends, please take your seats."

The audience quieted down.

"I would like to bring your attention to a change in our program." The conductor motioned to Autumn to take center stage. "Andrea, would you be so kind as to join your sister?"

Andrea looked perplexed, but nodded. She left her seat and walked up next to Autumn.

The conductor continued, "We learned this week that this is the last year our fair city will have the very talented Autumn and Andrea as residents."

Several in the audience voiced their disappointment.

"Did you tell?" Emma whispered to her grandmother.

"No, but you know there are no secrets in small towns, honey."

That's for sure.

"Autumn and Andrea are moving with their mother to Wilde, Nevada, at the end of the school year." The conductor looked at her girls. "Would you give us the pleasure of a duet?"

The audience applauded.

Emma smiled. She was so proud of Autumn and Andrea.

Adam leaned over. "They must be really talented for this kind of response."

"Just wait and see."

Autumn turned to Andrea. "Okay?"

Andrea smiled and winked at Bane and Adam. "Yes. I would love to."

"Did you see your daughter wink at us?" Adam was clearly thrilled.

Her girls spoke softly to each other.

Andrea went to the piano. "We will be performing 'Flight of the Bumblebee' by Nikolai Rimsky-Korsakov."

"That's a very difficult piece," Bane said.

Emma nodded. "Yes, it is."

Autumn brought her violin up to her chin and held her bow just above the strings. Andrea played the introduction and Autumn joined in, both their hands flying over their instruments so very fast, but never missing a single note.

The audience members were as still as statues, engrossed in the music her daughters were performing.

When the piece came to a climactic end, everyone stood, clapping.

Bane and Adam were on their feet, cheering "bravo," clearly surprised by Autumn and Andrea's talent.

The audience would not quiet down, continuing to applaud for her girls.

The conductor turned to Autumn and Andrea. "Young ladies, would you consider giving us one more?"

Autumn nodded and held up her instrument. "Ladies and gentlemen, prepare to be amazed. My sister and I are going to magically turn this violin into a fiddle."

Andrea smiled. "One. Two. Three. Four."

The hall erupted into cheers as they played a fast country song. The other students on the stage put down their instruments, moved behind the girls and began line dancing.

Her grandmother leaned over. "Just like my favorite television show with Rachel and Mr. Schue."

The whole audience clearly couldn't contain their excitement, as everyone was line dancing at their seats, including Bane and Adam.

When the song concluded, the crowd erupted once again into applause.

Emma looked into her girl's eyes and saw how happy they were. Suddenly, the looks on their faces changed as their gazes went past her to the back.

She turned around and saw Larry heading her direction. *As usual, he's missed all the excitement.*

* * * *

Adam sat on Emma's grandparents' sofa, listening to Autumn and Andrea play another song for him and Bane. He couldn't get over how much the girls looked like Emma, who was in the kitchen with her grandparents and Larry.

It was clear to him that Em's ex was tolerated more than welcomed in this house. Autumn and Andrea didn't seem interested in Larry at all, and he didn't seem interested in them or their music either.

Probably just another deadbeat dad. What a fool. Andrea and Autumn are incredible.

He was amazed at how gifted the girls were, and by the look on Bane's face, he was, too. Quietly, he leaned over to his brother. "When Wilde finds out about these girls, Autumn and Andrea will be playing at all the gatherings around town."

Bane nodded. "That's for sure."

When the girls ended their song, he and Bane jumped to their feet and clapped, yelling, "Encore. Encore."

Autumn and Andrea ran up to him and Bane, giving them sweet hugs.

"Amazing," Bane said.

He agreed. "God, you two are so unbelievably talented. Will you play another song for us?"

Andrea stepped back and smiled. "Thank you. We would love to. We enjoy playing for you very much."

Autumn, still holding on tight, said, "You're the best audience we've ever had." She turned to her sister. "Before we play another song, let's bring down some of our trophies to show them."

"Only if they would like to see them." Andrea turned to him and Bane. "Would you?"

He loved how happy the girls seemed. "Absolutely."

"That's a great idea," Bane added.

Autumn released him and Bane. "We'll be right back."

Andrea smiled. "Don't go anywhere."

He smiled back at her. "We're not going anywhere until we have a slice of your grandmother's famous chocolate pie you've been telling us about."

As they ascended up the stairs, Andrea turned back. "We helped make it."

Hearing the pride in her voice made him smile. "Then I'm sure I will love it, sweetheart. I hope I get at least two slices."

The girls laughed and vanished from sight.

When they were out of earshot, Bane turned to him. "Didn't you find it strange that Larry suggested we come here for pie? It's clear he's not a favorite of Emma's grandparents."

"I did think it was odd, bro. He's quite brazen, don't you think?"

Bane nodded. "I wonder if he was the reason Emma reacted the way she did to the phone call back home."

"I was wondering the same thing at the concert, but she doesn't seem frightened by him."

"No she doesn't."

"I'm betting Leland and Helen have a few things to say about Larry."

"I'm sure you're right." Bane sighed. It was clear that he, like him, wanted to protect not only Emma, but also the girls. "If we can get Helen and Leland away from the bastard for a minute or two I'm sure they will open up. I don't trust the guy, Adam."

"Neither do I, Bane. Neither do I."

Chapter Twelve

Emma leaned against Adam. "If you need a break, I can drive, too."

Adam had just taken over the wheel from Bane. "We've got it covered, baby."

"But, guys, we're going back to Wilde without stopping." They'd all agreed to drive straight through so that she could take some extra time to unpack and set up her new home. Bane and Adam were going to help her there, too. They were her dreams come true. "We're all beat from packing up my apartment."

Bane squeezed her hand. "We'll keep it in mind."

"Don't just keep it in mind, let me take over the driving for at least a couple of hours. It's not fair for me to just sit back and enjoy the trip."

They both laughed.

"Okay, honey. You can take over when we hit Casper," Adam said.

Bane grinned. "Em, you sure have a lot of fire inside you."

"You've only seen a small portion of my blaze, guys."

"Really?" Adam smiled. "Sounds like we have a lot more to look forward to with you, sub."

She grinned, anxious for them to show her more about BDSM. They'd even promised to take her to The Masters' Chambers once they believed she was ready. She vowed to herself to learn fast. The club would be a kind of graduation for her into the life that they'd been in for several years.

"I'm so excited about everything. I can't wait to get the girls to

Wilde and get started on my new job. You guys have been so wonderful. Autumn and Andrea really took a liking to you."

"Two handsome Marines. What's not to like?" Adam laughed. "They stole our hearts, Em."

Bane nodded. "You've done an amazing job with your girls. And all alone."

"I saw you talking to my grandparents. They must've told you about how absent Larry has been."

"They sure did," Adam said. "How is he reacting to you moving the girls to Wilde?"

"Honestly, I'm not sure he gives a damn. It really is strange how he has shown up lately. I can't seem to figure it out."

"My gut tells me he can't be trusted." Bane turned to her. "How long were you married to him?"

"Two awfully long years. I was only sixteen when I found out I was pregnant. He was twenty-six."

Bane cursed. "The son of a bitch should be in prison. You were a minor."

"I wasn't old enough to make good decisions. When Larry said he would marry me, I thought I didn't have another choice."

"The bastard probably only married you to keep from going to jail."

"Bane, you sound like my grandfather when I came back with a wedding ring on my finger. I thought he was going to kill Larry."

"I knew I liked your grandfather, Em," he said.

"Leland and Helen are true blue, that's for sure," Adam agreed. "How were you able to get married, Em? Didn't you need your mother's consent? Norma wasn't the kind of woman who would've given it to someone like Larry."

"You're right about that." She closed her eyes, recalling that tear-filled day she'd tied the knot with Larry. "My ex forged my mother's signature. I should've known better, but I didn't. I felt trapped and without any other options. I thought my baby needed a daddy. Mine died when I was so young. I felt like I'd lost out. I didn't want that for my child."

Bane squeezed her hand. "Honey, that's so understandable."

"That's what Mom told me when she found out. She never cared for Larry, but Mom finally did give her consent to our marriage, though after the fact. Like me, she hoped he would prove to be a good father. Mom and I were both wrong. I was so foolish back then. I should've listened to my mom and grandparents."

"You were very young, sweetheart, with a very big problem." Adam's words were so kind.

"For the next two years, I lived with the cheating bastard. It wasn't that I loved him. I just hoped he would take care of my girls and me. He didn't. He would always come home drunk with stale perfume on his clothes. I finally had enough and moved in with my grandparents until I could save the money I needed to get us our own place."

"According to your grandparents, you got your degree, too. God, Em, you're superwoman."

"Don't believe them. I'm not even close."

"Stop downplaying what you've accomplished, darlin'." Adam's tone was firm but kind. "You did what you had to do to get by. It's clear your two girls mean the world to you. You're amazing."

"He's right, sweetheart." Bane kissed her on the cheek. "You're incredible."

For a brief second, she almost believed what they saw in her.

Should I tell them about the voices?

God, she wanted to, but even though she'd promised to tell them sometime, she just couldn't bring herself to admit to them how flawed she really was right now. Not yet at least.

Time for a subject change. "Guys, shouldn't we stop and grab a bite to eat? I could use a break and a chance to stretch my legs."

"I saw a sign that said the best steaks in Wyoming are just a few miles up the road." Adam placed his right hand on her knee. "I'm hungry, too."

"You're always hungry, bro." Bane laughed. "But so am I."

God, they made her feel so good, so happy. "Maybe when we get back to Wilde I can organize a rematch on the pie-eating contest for you two."

"Not unless it's your grandma's pies, Em."

"Don't underestimate my abilities in the kitchen, guys. She and my mom taught me everything I know, and believe me I know a lot." She giggled, thinking about the first meal she would serve them in her new house. "From now on, you may call me Chef Em."

"Well, I for one, can't wait to try your cooking, Chef Em baby." Bane smiled.

"I for two, Chef Em baby." Adam laughed. "My favorite pie is apple."

"And yours, Bane?"

"Same, honey. I mean, Chef Em baby. We are twins, you know."

* * * *

Bane saw the familiar sign on Old Highway 93 that told him they were almost home.

13 Miles to Wilde, Nevada – population 969, we welcome you with 1,938 arms.

Emma had nodded off five minutes after they'd left the steakhouse and had remained fast asleep between him and Adam ever since.

"Should be back in town in under an hour, bro," Adam said softly.

"Yep. We will roll in around zero-four hundred."

"The diner will be open. I'm hungry again."

"Me, too. I bet when Chef Em wakes up that she'll be hungry." Adam smiled. "For pancakes."

They both laughed quietly, trying not to disturb Emma.

"Bane, can you believe she's slept nine hours straight?"

"No wonder. She worked like a dog back at her apartment."

"She's something special, that's for sure." Adam sighed. "I absolutely want to protect her from whatever she's afraid of."

"We're on the same page. I can't get the image of how she reacted to that phone call out of my head." He'd played it over and over in his mind. "I know she said her reaction had nothing to do with Larry, but I'm going to protect her and her girls from him no matter what."

"Definitely," Adam said. "The sooner we get Autumn and Andrea to Wilde the better."

"School will be out for them in a few more weeks. I know Emma's grandparents won't let anything happen to them. They don't trust Larry either."

"Em's granddad told me that every time Larry comes over to visit the girls he makes himself at home like it's his own house."

"That bastard missed the girls' duet." Bane had only been around those two angels for a few hours and already bonded with them. "Once Autumn and Andrea are in Wilde with Em, I doubt the fucker will come around anymore."

"And if he does, you and I will be here to make sure he doesn't hurt their little hearts again."

"Did you see how they reacted whenever he was in the room?"

"I did." Adam frowned. "He's a total stranger to his own daughters."

"They deserve better, bro. Them and their wonderful mother."

"I want to be that for them."

Bane nodded. "Me, too." He spotted Carlotta's Liquor Store and Tarot Card Reading Room up ahead. "Time to wake Em so she'll be ready to have some breakfast with us."

"I'm on it." Adam gently nudged their beautiful passenger.

Em yawned and opened her eyes. "Is it my turn to drive already?"

"Yes, sweetheart." Bane placed his hand on her leg. "Let me pull over so you can take the wheel for the last mile."

"Last mile?" Her eyes widened. "How long have I been asleep?"

Adam kissed her. "As long as you needed, baby. Like we've told you before, we're here for you. Always."

Chapter Thirteen

Emma held the front door open to her new home. "Go get some rest."

Bane and Adam looked totally exhausted. They'd been so stubborn.

"Are you sure there isn't something else we need to do for you, baby?" Adam asked with a yawn.

"I'm sure. Every box is unpacked. Everything is put away. All my furniture is in place. You've even helped me put up photos of my girls and grandparents on the hallway wall, making sure their frames are all level. You both are wonderful and I appreciate all you've done for me. But like I've been saying since breakfast, you need to get some sleep. You are meeting with your new FBI boss in the morning. You need to be fresh."

"What about you?" Adam asked. "I heard you talking on the phone with Mac. You told her you were going to come in tomorrow instead of taking the whole week."

"Why not? There's nothing left to do here."

Bane wrapped his arms around her. "We all need some rest, sweetheart. I could use a shower, some clean clothes, and a few hours of shut-eye." He kissed her tenderly. "We'll be back to take you to dinner tonight and maybe we can rent a movie."

"That sounds great." She didn't want to be away from them for too long. "I think we could all use a very low-key evening."

"Maybe so." Adam stroked her hair. "Or maybe we could pick up where we left off at the hotel in Casper? What do you say, sub?"

"That depends on if you two Doms get some much-needed rest or not." She grinned. "Or it's 'pancakes' for both of you."

Adam smiled and pressed his lips to hers. "You better rest up, too, sweetheart. I've got some things I want to introduce you to tonight."

He and Bane left, and she shut the door.

Emma looked around her new home and smiled. "It's perfect."

"No, Sis. It's not." Lily's voice rang out throughout the house.

Emma brought her hands up, covering her ears. "God, no. Not again."

"Yes, again, Emma." Samantha's tone echoed off the walls. "Again and again and again. You will never be free of us. Never."

"Stop it. Why won't you leave me alone?"

"We will never leave you alone. You are our sister. You are just like us."

Her heart raced violently in her chest. "I'm nothing like you. Go away. Please. Just leave me alone."

Her cell rang and she jumped, feeling completely panicked.

She glanced at the caller ID. *Larry? Is something wrong with Autumn and Andrea?* "Larry. Are the girls okay?"

"Of course they're okay. Emma, what's wrong?"

Horrified that her worst nightmare was coming true, she blurted out, "Voices. Larry, I'm hearing voices." Her eyes welled up. "I am losing my mind just like my sisters."

"I don't quite understand what's going on, sweetheart, but I am here for you. I'll make sure you're okay, Em."

Larry had never called her "Em" before. Only Bane and Adam had. Somehow, being called by that nickname made her feel a little bit better, a little bit safer. "I need you to be there for our girls. You can't screw up anymore." She choked back her tears as she imagined herself living without her daughters, but what other choice did she have?

"Whatever you need me to be, I swear I will be."

"You better." She would have to say good-bye to her girls. They deserved a life free of insanity, a life of happiness and possibilities. *Not a mother like me who is about to go off the deep end completely.*

Samantha and Lily had seemed normal for years and had ended up killing people close to them. Emma couldn't imagine herself capable of harming anyone, especially Autumn or Andrea. *But what if I'm wrong? What if the madness overtakes me?*

I can't trust myself. I must say good-bye to my precious girls.

Tears rolled down her cheeks. *God help me. Being without them is going to kill me.*

"I know you and I had our rough times, but I never stopped loving you and our girls."

"Don't, Larry. It's been over for years. You and I will never be together again."

"Okay, Em. Whatever you say." Larry had never sounded like this before, so understanding. "I'll be there for the girls. I swear."

She would also have to end it with Bane and Adam. It would take every ounce of courage and would rip her heart to shreds, but she must break it off with them now. She couldn't drag anyone else down with her.

"Are you still there, Emma?"

She took a deep breath, bracing herself for the good-byes ahead. "Yes."

"Why don't you come back to North Dakota and we can work this all out together?"

"No. I'm never going back there. Ever."

* * * *

Adam couldn't bring himself to get out of the bed, though he'd been awake for a little while. He'd fallen instantly asleep after his shower.

He glanced over at the clock and smiled. Less than an hour before he would be with the woman of his dreams again. He hoped Emma had crawled into bed herself shortly after he and Bane had left. Tonight, he had big plans for her.

Bane came in with his cell in his hand. "Em's on speaker. She wanted to talk to both of us."

He swung his legs to the floor. "Hey, sweetheart."

"Hi, Adam. I'm too tired to go to dinner tonight." There was something in her tone that didn't sound right to him.

"That's okay," Bane said. "Adam and I can go get takeout and bring it over to your house."

He nodded to his brother. "We can stay in all night, Em. Just relax."

"I really would like to be alone this evening, if you don't mind." Her voice was shaky. "And I know you two need more sleep. Thank you so much for all you've done for me. I can't ever thank you enough."

This sounds like a breakup call. "Em, we're coming over now." He pulled on his boots.

"What's wrong, baby?" Bane was onto something. "Did you get another phone call that upset you?"

"No. Not a phone call."

"Then what, sweetheart?" He hated to hear her sound so frightened. "It's time you told us."

"I–I have been avoiding this call for the past few hours, pacing around my house. This is hard, but you deserve to know everything. It's only fair." There was sadness in every syllable she uttered, crushing him and Bane. "I guess face-to-face is how it should be. It's only right after all you've done for me."

"Honey, just stay put," Bane said. "We have no idea what is bothering you, but we will always be there for you."

"I know you want to be, but it just wouldn't be right."

Adam felt his gut tighten. No way were they going to let her end it. Something was behind this sudden change in her. It was past time to get to the bottom of her fears. "Em, we'll be there as fast as we can."

* * * *

Emma clicked off her cell. She couldn't stop trembling. How was she going to live without Bane and Adam? She'd already fallen in love with them, and for a while the voices had gone away. But now her mind was cracking again.

"I've got to be brave. I've got to do the right thing," she said aloud to herself, trying to gather her courage. "I have to break it off with them. It's the only way. As much as I want to be with them, they deserve better than me. A crazy person."

"Listen to her, Lily." Samantha's voice returned, chilling her to the bone. "She's finally admitting it."

Her sister's maniacal laughter rang throughout the house.

"You're just like us, Emma," Lily said. "Just. Like. Us."

"No. No. I am not."

"We're sisters. Family. Like copies of each other."

"It's not true. I'm nothing like you and Samantha. Go away."

"We will never leave you." Samantha's cackling got louder and louder.

"Please, God. No." She couldn't take it anymore. She had to get away.

"We have work for you to do, Emma," Lily said. "People that need to pay for their crimes against us. You can't imagine how powerful you will feel the first time you watch someone die by your own hands."

"Emma, you will know very soon how amazing it feels to kill," Samantha said.

"Stop it. Get out of my head. I won't. I couldn't."

"Yes, you will. Sam and I will make sure of it."

"No. No. No. I will not hurt anyone. Ever." She looked around the room, expecting to see wispy images of her two dead sisters. "I am not alone. Bane and Adam made you go away. They will again." *I need them.*

"Those two idiots you've been fucking can't drive us away," Lily said. "We're here to stay."

Samantha mocked, "Forever and ever and ever and *ever.*"

Emma brought her hands up to her ears, but her sister's chant never ended. In a complete panic and unable to stand another second hearing them, she ran out of the house and into Bane and Adam's embrace.

* * * *

Bane and his brother held Emma tight between them. It was obvious by her tremors that something had scared her to death. "Baby, it's okay. We are here."

"You are safe with us," Adam whispered to her.

"I–I…they were…inside…"

His gut tightened. Had there been an intruder? Other than being shaken up, Em looked fine. *If anyone harmed a single hair on her head, I will kill them.*

Adam released her and ran into the house. Bane knew he was going to check it out.

"Shh, sweetheart." He cupped her chin. "You can tell us all about it once you catch your breath."

It took several minutes of consoling Emma for her to relax enough to talk coherently. "I'm okay now, Bane."

Clearly, she wasn't. "Was someone in your house?"

"No."

Adam came out and gave him the thumbs-up that all was clear inside. "Are you feeling better now, Em?"

She nodded. "Yes. They never bother me when you're here."

They?

Bane held her tight. "Who never bothers you, sweetheart?"

She closed her eyes. "I hear my dead sisters' voices."

Adam came up behind her, wrapping her up between them. "It's okay."

"I have been hearing my sisters' voices ever since Mom and Lily's funeral. Lily and Samantha say I'm just like them. Our father went crazy. They went crazy. Now, I'm going crazy."

Bane knew this had something to do with her reaction to the phone call the other day. "Honey, did you hear their voices through your cell?"

"Only once. It happened right before you picked me up at the hotel to go shopping for the present for Shelby's baby."

He remembered how engrossed Emma had been when they'd found her in the lobby. Staring at her cell's screen, she hadn't even realized they were right next to her. "That's why you jumped when Autumn called that night."

"Yes. I thought it was going to be one of my sisters on the other end."

"Did you check the caller ID, baby?" Adam asked.

She nodded. "It was unknown."

He kissed her forehead.

She smiled weakly. "Who knows who called me that day? Maybe it was a wrong number or a telemarketer, but I thought I heard my sisters' voices. It's all in my head. I've only heard their voices once on the phone, but I have heard them several times through the walls in my apartment back in North Dakota. And now I'm hearing them here in Wilde." She pointed to the rental house. "I thought I could start a new life here. I didn't expect the voices to follow me. But they did. I'm going crazy. I wanted to tell you before this, before now, before I fell in love with you, but I just couldn't bring myself to. Can you ever forgive me?"

"Em, there is nothing to forgive. You weren't the only one who fell in love. You're the most wonderful, beautiful woman I've ever known. I love you." Bane pressed his lips to hers, hoping to take away her fears, to make her feel safe. "Trust me, you are not going crazy."

Adam turned her around and locked his eyes on hers. "I love you, Em. You have my heart in your hands. And Bane is definitely right about you—you are perfectly sane. You've been through so much the past several months and all on your own. Your sister murdered your mother in cold blood. Trauma like that can cause all kinds of things to happen to a person. No wonder you think you're hearing voices. Trust me, it will pass. You just need a little time and you don't need to be alone anymore."

He stroked her hair, feeling her trembles. "Em, do you want to go back in the house, or do you want us to take you somewhere else?"

She took a deep breath, and he and Adam could see her strength returning. "It's my house. Yes. I want to go back inside. I won't be driven out by my own delusions. Besides, when I'm with you I never hear the voices."

There's something about this whole thing that just doesn't add up.

"Adam was right. You don't ever need to be alone." He led her to the front door. "And we're going to make sure you never are again."

* * * *

Adam listened to Emma's steady breathing. He and Bane had her between them on the bed.

They'd held and listened to her until she'd finally relaxed. Now that she was completely out, he leaned up on his elbow and said quietly to his brother, "None of this makes any sense to me."

"You're reading my mind, Adam."

"We've been around many soldiers who have been traumatized and have PTSD. They're all withdrawn. There's nothing withdrawn about Emma. In fact, she's just the opposite."

"I know. And what about that call she told us about? Ghosts don't use cell phones to contact the living. I want to get that checked out first thing with Caleb."

"Agreed. Plus, we need to run a thorough sweep of this house."

"After we escort her to the television station, we can bring Caleb back here and go through every inch of this place."

"Bane, she's the one for us. The only one."

"I know. She's ours. It's our job to get to the bottom of this."

"She deserves our very best." Adam looked down at the woman who had changed his world. He would go into the bowels of hell itself and fight every devil the place contained to make sure Emma was safe.

Chapter Fourteen

Emma got out of the vehicle and turned to the two wonderful men who'd rescued her from the voices once again.

What was it about Bane and Adam that made her feel so safe? *Everything.*

They could be so gentle and kind under all that toughness. They'd listened to her almost all night. When she'd told them about her worry for her girls, they'd helped her through the worst of her fears. They'd talked to her about what trauma on the battlefield could do and how they'd seen fellow soldiers overcome the pain.

Time. That's what they said I needed. Time and understanding.

They'd given her their understanding and had promised to give her all the time she needed. The voices hadn't returned. She was filled with hope because of her two amazing Marines. Whatever demons she had to face she didn't have to face them alone ever again.

"When do you guys have to turn this truck back in?"

"After our meeting with Caleb, sweetheart," Bane said.

Adam held her hand. "We've got it covered."

They walked her to the front door of the television station.

"I've got it from here, guys."

Bane pulled her into his arms. "Are you sure you'll be okay while we're gone?"

"I'm sure. Plus I have both your numbers in my phone in case I need you."

Bane kissed her tenderly. "I love you, baby."

Before she could catch her breath, Adam gave her another kiss. "I love you, darlin'."

"I love you both. Now go. You don't want to be late on your first day with the FBI."

"We'll be back to pick you up at five," Bane said firmly.

"I'll be here."

After they left, she walked into the station, praying the voices would never return.

* * * *

Larry watched the two bastards drive away from the television station.

Those interfering motherfuckers messed up everything.

Though an aggravation, it was necessary to return to Nevada to keep his plan on track. The timeline had changed, and he must act now. After hearing the assholes' plan to sweep Emma's house, he'd driven all night to Wilde.

He stepped out of the bushes and dusted off his suit.

Now was his chance to get Emma alone.

Those Marines think they're smart, but I'm smarter.

Even having to rush things, all the pieces were in place. Just like when she was sixteen, the bitch would be putty in his hands.

He sent the text to the mimic slut that would get the ball rolling.

* * * *

Sitting in her new office, Emma took the paperwork from Mac.

"These are for your employee file," her boss said. "You know. Insurance. Contact information. That kind of thing. Take your time filling it out. I've got to run over to Studio B where we're taping a cooking show. All hands on deck for this one. Mary Wilde is making one of her signature recipes today and we're setting up now. Adara is our receptionist. She's out getting the ingredients Mary requested. While you're finishing up your paperwork, I hope you don't mind answering the phone until Adara gets back, which won't be long."

"I don't mind at all."

"I don't expect any calls or any visitors. Once she's back, I want you to come to Studio B to observe."

"Sounds great."

"Once we're finished shooting, I'll give you the tour of the whole place. Then we can sit down and talk."

"I am so excited to be working for you, Mac. Thank you."

Mac stood. "No. Thank you. You're a lifesaver, Em."

After Mac left, Emma's cell rang.

She answered it and heard the horrific voices again.

* * * *

Bane pushed the piece of paper with Emma's cell phone number over to Caleb.

"How long before you know where this call originated from?" Adam asked.

"I'm pretty sure I can do better than that. I bet I can tell you who made the call." Their new boss looked at the paper and pulled out his cell. "There's a new CIA team in Destiny, Colorado, that I've been working with. Jena is one of their lead techs and she can hack into anything. With Emma's number and the date and time of the call, I think Jena can have an answer for us in ten minutes."

"Tell her to make it five."

Caleb nodded. "Will do."

* * * *

Emma threw the phone to the floor. "No. No. No. This can't be happening."

"What can't be happening, Em?" Larry stood in the doorway to her office holding a folder. "Are you hearing them again?"

"W–What are you doing here?" She closed her eyes and took a deep breath.

He bent down and retrieved her damaged cell. "We need to talk."

"How did you know where to find me?"

"I stopped in at your mom's old diner. One of the waitresses told me you were working here. There was no one in the front office, so I made myself at home and looked around until I found you. Nameplate on the door. Very nice, Em. Big job. Good for you."

"I know you didn't come all the way from North Dakota to congratulate me, Larry. What do you want to talk about?"

"I told you I would be there for you and our girls and I meant it." Larry sat down in the chair Mac had just vacated ten minutes ago.

Emma's heart was thudding in her chest and in her temples. The voices had returned soon after Bane and Adam had dropped her off. She didn't know why her two Marines were able to keep her dead sisters at bay, but somehow they were. But she knew even if the guys agreed to be with her twenty-four hours a day, that wasn't really possible. That wasn't living. They had jobs with the FBI. They had goals and dreams. Her goals would never be realized. Her dreams had all turned to nightmares.

Larry held out her cell to her. "Have a seat, honey."

She sat down without taking back her phone. *I never want to touch that thing again.*

He placed it and the folder on her desk. "Em, you need help."

"I know that, Larry."

"I've got a friend who works with people with mental illness. He is employed at the state hospital."

She shook her head. "I already told you I'm not going back to North Dakota."

"I know you did, but Em, you and I both know what happened to your sisters." He reached across the desk for her hand, but she pulled it back. "Think about our girls."

She swallowed hard. "What about them?"

"That's a very good question. Have you considered that you might be a threat to Autumn and Andrea in your current state? Samantha and Lily were perfectly sane and then they weren't. It could be happening to you." Larry opened the folder and revealed the legal documents inside. "I had my attorney draw these up after our call when you told me about what you had been going through."

She glanced down at the paperwork. "You want full custody of our girls?"

"You and I know it's for the best for now until you get better. Your grandparents are great with the girls but they can't be stand-in parents for you and me."

She looked up at him. "Larry, this can't be one of your fly-by-night promises."

He smiled. "It won't be, baby. I've grown up. I know what I want."

"What do you want?"

"I want to be a dad to our daughters. And if I can't be your husband again, I want to be your friend. Sign the papers. Let me take you to my buddy at the state hospital and get you checked out fully."

"I don't know, Larry. I'm not sure what the right thing to do is."

"Look at the paragraph where I return custody to you. This is only temporary, Em. Once you're well and over this speed bump in your life, you can come back to this town and start again. Please. For our girls. Sign the papers."

She scanned the entire document. *What choice do I have?* She grabbed a pen.

* * * *

Adam looked at the time on his phone again. It had been only four minutes since Caleb had gotten in touch with the woman in Destiny, but every second felt like an eternity. Patience had never been his strong suit.

Caleb's cell buzzed. "That's her. Hi, Jena."

He and Bane leaned forward, hanging on every word.

"Thanks. I owe you one." Their boss clicked off the phone. "You were right. It came from North Dakota. The caller was a Mr. Larry Grant."

* * * *

Emma brought the pen down to the signature line of the custody papers Larry had given her.

Her hand shook. She looked up at her ex.

He was leaning forward in the chair with a slight smile on his face.

Her grandmother's warning about Larry came flashing back into her mind. *"Mark my words, Emma. He's up to something. I don't trust him. The one thing I'm glad about you moving to Wilde is, Larry will likely never see Autumn and Andrea again."*

Her grandmother's instincts had never been wrong before.

What am I doing? I don't want to sign away custody of my girls.

Bane and Adam had helped quiet the voices. They'd helped her believe in a chance that things were going to be okay. It might not be easy, but she now knew it was possible. Her two amazing men had promised to help her. *I will be fine.*

She placed the pen back on the desk and pushed the unsigned paperwork away. "Larry, I can't do this."

"What do you mean you can't do this? It's for the best. It's your only choice."

"But you're wrong, Larry. I do have choices. I'm not sixteen anymore. I'm a grown woman who can make decisions on her own."

"This is ridiculous." Larry's tone turned harsh. "You're making a big mistake, Emma."

"You've only been coming back around the girls for a few short weeks. You even missed their duet when you knew exactly what time Autumn's concert was. You can't keep doing that. You can't keep being late and making excuses. If you want to be in the girls' lives, then you have a lot to prove. You are still a stranger to them. There is absolutely no way I could ever turn over custody of my girls to you. I'm their mother. It's my job to protect them. You must understand that?"

"I understand more than you know." Larry placed the paperwork neatly back into the folder and tucked it under his arm. "I didn't want to do this the hard way, but you are leaving me no choice."

She stood up. "Are you thinking about taking me to court to try to win custody of our girls? You'll lose, Larry. Trust me on that. They are mine."

He laughed. "I don't want those two little bitches, Emma. They are so much like you it makes me sick."

Shocked at his words, she screamed, "Get out of my office, you son of a bitch. Get out now."

He pulled out a gun and pointed it at her. "Actually, we are both going to leave right now."

* * * *

Bane turned to Adam. "Let's get Em."

"Go," Caleb said. "I'll get on the horn with the authorities in North Dakota about Larry Grant."

Rage fueled his every step as he and Adam ran to the truck. Emma's ex had been responsible for the call that had left her shaken. The fucker was certainly responsible for all of it. Why? That would have to be sorted out later. For now, he and Adam needed to get to Emma.

* * * *

Emma walked out of the television station. There wasn't a single person anywhere to be seen.

Larry held a pistol to her back. "My car is straight ahead. We'll get in on the passenger's side and you will slide over to the driver's seat."

"Where are you taking me?"

"To your rental house. Now shut the fuck up and move." He poked her hard with the barrel of his gun. "Or I'll shoot you and our daughters will be orphans."

Oh God, no. Please. She'd never really trusted him, though she had hoped he would change for the girls. He'd always been so self-absorbed. "What's this all about? You don't want to do this. Please."

"This is your fault, Emma. I tried to make it as easy as possible for you, but you didn't let me. Keep moving."

When they were in the car, he handed her the ignition key. "Start the engine."

"Why are you doing this, Larry?"

"Drive, bitch." With the barrel of his gun poking her in the side, he tossed the custody papers to the backseat. "Once we get to your house, you fucking cunt, I can't wait to tell you all the hard work I've done. It's brilliant."

* * * *

Adam ran into the station with Bane.

"May I help you?" the woman behind the receptionist desk asked.

"Emma Grant. Where's her office?"

"I can buzz her for you."

"Adara, where is Emma?" Mac came out of an office holding a damaged cell phone.

It's Emma's phone. Fuck. "Bane, the son of a bitch must've called her again with the voices."

"Yes." His brother's face was full of rage.

Mac stepped up to them. "Voices? What voices?"

"No time to explain." *Does the bastard have Emma?* His gut tightened at the thought. "Do you have any idea where she is?"

"She was supposed to come back to the studio when Adara got back."

"Em is in trouble, Mac. Call us if she returns." He and Bane ran out the door. His heart was pounding hard in his chest. "We've got to find her. Let's try her house first."

"Yes. I'll call Caleb." Bane brought out his phone as they jumped into the truck. "He can put out an APB on Larry. He and Sheriff Champion can check the diner and other places in town."

He and Bane had rescued many fellow soldiers on hundreds of battlefields against thousands of enemies. They'd been called heroes, though they never felt much like heroes. They were only doing their duty.

As he hit the gas, Adam knew he'd never wanted to rescue anyone more than now. He and Bane would give their lives to save Emma, their one true love.

* * * *

Emma kept twisting her hands, trying to free herself of the duct tape Larry had used to fasten her wrists and ankles to the chair.

He placed the gun on the counter. "Place looks nice, Emma. Too bad you won't live long enough to enjoy it."

Every part of her tensed and her heart skipped several beats. "I don't understand this, Larry. You said you don't want the girls. It doesn't make any sense. Why are you doing this to me?"

"Because you gave me no choice. Do you have a stepladder, Emma?"

"Yes, why?" She needed to keep her cool with him if she was going to survive this.

"So many questions." He reached for the pistol. "Remember who has the gun here, Emma."

She nodded, continuing to attempt to free herself without his knowledge. "I remember. There's a stepladder in the garage."

"You want to get me out of your sight so you can try to break free? You're not as dumb as you were when we were married. Good for you. I'll use a chair." He pulled one out and pushed it to the wall. "You want to know what this is about. You're ex is a genius, that's what."

He climbed on the chair and took off the air vent in the kitchen. He reached in the duct and pulled out some things she didn't recognize.

"What are those?"

"These are how your sisters were able to talk to you." He laughed. "Genius, right?"

"You? You were the one behind the voices."

He laughed wickedly. "You're not going crazy, Em. I just needed you to think you were." He held up the jumble of wires he'd pulled out of her vent. "Surveillance equipment that I modified with speakers for my purposes. There are more in all your vents."

She was shocked at what he was saying. "Why, Larry?"

"It was plan A, which I much preferred. In that plan you didn't have to die. You only had to be committed. But when you refused to sign the papers, I had to go to plan B. I have to be in charge of the girls."

Oh God, no. He's crazy. I don't want him near my girls ever again.

He put the vent back in place, stepped off the chair, and placed the equipment he'd retrieved on the kitchen table. "I can get the rest after I take care of you."

She didn't like the sound of that one bit. "My boss is going to miss me at work."

"I'm sure she will. And those two fuckers you've been sleeping with will, too. By the time they come around, I'll be long gone." He pulled out a glass from her cabinet and filled it with water. "I'm about to become a very wealthy man."

"What money? You're not making any sense."

He grinned and pulled out several prescription bottles from his coat pocket and placed them next to the water glass. "Your grandparents' land is sitting on top of one of the largest oil reserves in the country. Now that you and the girls are their only heirs, I knew what I had to do. That's why we are here. After Helen and Leland learn about your suicide, they will be devastated. That will give me an opening. They will welcome my help with the girls. After a few days, I'll be able to set the ball in motion to take them out. No one will question the deaths of two old fucks, especially when I make it look like it came from a gas leak. Like you, Emma, they will die peacefully in their sleep. Yours from pills and theirs from carbon monoxide poisoning."

He grabbed the pills and the glass of water and stepped in front of her. "Once you take your last breath, I'll remove the duct tape and place you in your bed. Whoever discovers your body will find the pills next to you and will assume you took your own life."

"Larry, you can't hurt the girls like this."

"Baby, don't worry about Autumn and Andrea. I'll make sure they go to the finest boarding school my money can buy. Be a good girl and open your mouth for me."

"You can't make me swallow those pills. I won't." She clamped her lips together, tightening her jaw.

"Goddamn it, Emma." He placed the glass on the table and poured out a fistful of pills into his hand. With his other hand, he pinched her nose. "Don't fight me. You've got to breathe sometime."

She held her breath for as long as she could. When she couldn't any longer and parted her lips, he shoved the pills in her mouth. She spit them in his face.

He slapped her hard. "You fucking bitch." He grabbed his gun. "Do that again and I will blow your head off."

The duct tape around her wrists seemed to be loosening. She needed more time. "Shoot me and this won't look like a suicide, Larry. It will ruin all your plans."

"If I have to hold you down to take these pills, I will."

"Wait. Let me at least write a note to say good-bye to Autumn and Andrea." *More time. Please.* Larry's gun would be within reach once her hands were free. "Please, Larry. Wouldn't a suicide note help seal the deal for your plan?"

"What do you take me for, Emma? A fool? I'm not untying you." He poured out another fistful of pills into his hand.

With all her might, she twisted her wrists and was able to free her hands. She didn't hesitate, but clawed at his face with one hand and reached for the gun with the other.

He shoved her and the chair to the ground before she got the pistol.

"Fuck you." He grabbed the gun and touched his face, which was bleeding from her scratches. He punched her, and pain shot through her jaw.

Her ankles were still attached to the legs of the chair, so she couldn't run. The whole world was on its side. She could see her front door though her vision was blurry.

Larry brought the barrel to her head. "Time to die, bitch."

The door opened and in ran her two Marines, guns firing.

Larry fell to the ground with a loud thud.

Bane and Adam ran to her, quickly releasing her legs from the chair.

"Are you okay, sweetheart?" Adam's concern was all over his face.

Bane bent over Larry's unmoving body.

She took a deep, calming breath. "I'm fine now that you and Bane are here."

Adam lifted her up into his arms.

"Larry is dead," Bane said flatly. "He's no longer a threat, sweetheart."

Adam kissed her on the cheek. "The fucker will never hurt you again, Em."

"Or my girls." She looked at them, the two men who had never given up on her. "The voices. They weren't real. I'm not going crazy."

Chapter Fifteen

Emma sat between Bane and Adam in Sheriff Champion's office. Bane had his arm around her and Adam held her hand.

Caleb, their FBI boss, sat in the chair closest to the sheriff, who was behind his desk.

"Are you sure you are ready for this, Emma?" Sheriff Champion asked.

"I'm fine. Your son is an excellent doctor." She'd learned that the sheriff had once been a physician himself.

"Yes, he is. I'm very proud of him. So no broken bones?"

"Alex checked me out and said I was good to go. The fact that I know I'm not losing my mind has given me such relief I feel I could do anything right now."

The sheriff smiled. "I'm glad."

Adam squeezed her hand. "We're all glad."

"Definitely." Bane kissed her on the cheek.

She felt completely safe in their arms.

"Let's get to it then." Sheriff Champion looked down at some paperwork on his desk. "We have your statement, Emma, and I want to fill you in on everything the authorities found back in North Dakota."

"I knew Larry wasn't a good guy and completely self-centered. That's why I left him all those years ago. But I never thought he would be capable of such horrible things."

"Greed sent him over the edge, Emma. When he learned about the oil reserve that would net millions to your grandparents, he conspired to make the money his." Caleb had a kind face. "After Jena had let us know that original call had come from Larry, I was able to get a warrant from the local authorities. The officers went to his house and found a woman who had been living with him for the past few months. Turns out that the woman is a performer whose specialty is imitating celebrities."

"Oh my God. That's why she sounded so much like my sisters."

Adam and Bane's boss nodded. "Apparently Larry had some videos of them that the woman had studied to get their voices right."

"I remember he made copies of several birthday videos of Autumn and Andrea when they were very young." She turned to Adam and Bane. "My sisters were in every single one of those videos. I thought Larry wanted the videos to remember the years he missed in the girls' lives. Turns out he only wanted to use them against me and my family."

Bane pulled her in tight. "He can't hurt you or the girls ever again, baby."

Adam asked Caleb and Sheriff Champion, "What happened to the mimic?"

"She's in jail for the scam awaiting trial," Caleb said.

"The officers who arrested her found more equipment in Larry's house similar to what we retrieved from your place." Sheriff Champion looked at the paperwork on his desk. "Our bet is your ex had planted the equipment originally in your apartment back in North Dakota. When you came to Wilde, you clearly messed up his plans. He had to resort to the cell phone to keep the voices coming at you until you got a place."

"When did Larry put that crap in my vents?"

"Jena helped us figure that one out, too. She found his name on a couple of flight manifests," Caleb said. "Larry flew to Wilde while you were headed with Bane and Adam to pack up your stuff. That way no one would know he had left the state. He arrived back in Minot and went straight to your daughter's concert."

She sighed, recalling him walking in as her girls were taking their bows. "That's why he was late."

"Exactly," Caleb said. "I have confirmed with some of my sources that your grandparents' land is rich with oil."

She now had a clear picture of what Larry had been scheming and how he'd gone about trying to destroy her. "I must call my grandparents and fill them in. I've got to get to my girls."

"Mackenzie already talked to the owners of the television station, Lance and Chuck." Bane smiled. "They've got their pilot and jet on standby ready to take all three of us to North Dakota."

"Wow. I haven't even put in a full day of work for them. That's so generous."

Sheriff Champion nodded. "Wilde has the best billionaires in the entire country."

"Not just billionaires, Sheriff." She looked around the room. "Everyone in Wilde has been so good to me. There isn't a better place for me to raise my girls than right here."

Chapter Sixteen

Back in North Dakota, Emma sat with her grandmother on the porch, looking out at the stars. The girls were asleep in their beds. Bane, Adam, and her grandfather were in the kitchen finishing off the last of the apple pie that her grandmother had baked for them.

"Grandma, I'm still shocked that the girls didn't have much of a reaction when I told them Larry was dead."

"I'm not. They didn't know him at all, thank God. He was a complete stranger. When he did come around, the girls felt awkward. Andrea's instincts were right all along."

"Yes, they were." Emma remembered her daughter saying she didn't like Larry when she was very young. "I can't get over how she is around Bane and Adam."

"I know. They sure do bring her out of her shell. She was laughing and carrying on during that card game they taught her and Autumn. Both your girls already adore your guys. I'm glad you told them you were dating. It's good you and your mom told them how things worked in Wilde. It didn't come as a shock. They are so thrilled you found love with Bane and Adam, and so are your grandpa and me. When do you three plan on heading back?"

"Tomorrow morning." She still couldn't believe there was a private jet waiting at the airport to zoom them all back to Wilde. "I'll come back and get the girls in a few weeks."

"Last day of school is June fourth, Emma. Maybe you, Bane, and Adam can stay a few days."

She reached over and grabbed her grandmother's hand. "I promise to visit as often as we can, but I would rather you and Grandpa move to Wilde."

"Sweetheart, didn't your grandpa tell you?"

"Tell me what?"

Her grandmother smiled. "We're going to buy a place in Wilde. We've got a few things to settle here before we do, but we don't want to be too far from you and the girls."

Her heart swelled with joy. "Really?"

"Yes, really. Leland has really bonded with Bane and Adam. He's excited about moving to Wilde as much as I am."

"What about the farm?"

"We've talked to your granddad's nephew, who is a great guy. He's going to move in with his lovely wife and kids and take care of the place for us. Besides, with our newfound wealth we can fly in and check on the place anytime we like."

Bane and Adam came out the front door.

She kissed her grandmother on the cheek. "I can't imagine being happier, Grandma."

"Would you ladies like to come in and play some cards?" Adam asked.

"Leland told us that he's the best player in the house with you, Helen, as a close second."

Her grandmother stood up and grinned. "That sounds like a challenge to me. What do you say, Emma? Shall we show our men what we're made of?"

"Absolutely, Grandma."

Chapter Seventeen

With a swirl of excitement and nervousness spinning inside her, Emma walked into The Masters' Chambers between her two Doms. She kept her eyes on them alone. That was what they'd instructed her to do.

They wore exactly the same clothing—leather pants, military boots, and T-shirt. They were the sexiest creatures she'd ever seen, and they were with her.

She glanced down at the outfit they'd bought for her for tonight—a long-sleeve lacy chemise, a thong, a bra, stilettos, and a ribbon around her throat—*everything black.*

Tonight, she was Bane and Adam's sub.

She wanted to make them proud. The practice at home had elevated her to states of ecstasy that she'd never dreamed possible. They'd taught her so much about their lifestyle, a lifestyle that was now hers, too. But this was her first time to walk into a BDSM club, and she was vibrating inside with anticipation.

I'm so wonderfully nervous.

After signing all the papers, they headed into their private room, though it wasn't completely private. There were windows in the room, where members could see inside from the hallway. Although they had blinds, they were currently opened.

"Sirs, are you going to close the blinds during our play?"

Bane walked over and shut the blinds. "For now, sub, we'll keep them closed."

For now?

The room's cinder brick walls were painted a dark red and the lighting perfectly enhanced the erotic feel of the space.

Adam placed the large leather bag on the floor next to the bench and sling. She believed he and Bane had brought a wide assortment of toys, but she hadn't seen what they'd packed in the bag for tonight's play. They'd told her they wanted to keep that a surprise.

"What do you think of your first visit to a dungeon, sub?" Adam asked.

"It's a bit intimidating, Sir, but red is my favorite color.

Hanging from the ceiling by four chains was a leather sling that reminded her a little of a hammock, though it was too small for someone to relax in. In front of the sling was a bench she recognized immediately from the books she'd read to be for spanking.

Adam walked in front of her and pulled her in close. He leaned down and pressed his lips to her. She came up on her toes, welcoming his kiss that gave her warmth and confidence.

He stepped back. "Remove your clothes, sub. Your Masters want to see your perfect body."

"Yes, Sir."

Their eyes were fixed on her, adding to the thrill. She removed the chemise.

Bane held out his hand, and she gave the chemise to him. He folded the garment and placed it neatly on the table.

A shiver ran up and down her spine as she unfastened her bra. She enjoyed giving them a show and loved their reactions to it.

Bane and Adam were flagrantly rubbing their hard cock through their leather pants.

I'm turning them on. Let's see if I can drive them wild.

Getting into the spirit of her striptease, she took her time removing her bra. She could see that her performance was having quite the impact on them. They seemed to be on the edge, having difficulty containing their lust.

She ran her fingers over her now exposed nipples and licked her lips, sending them a naughty glance.

"Damn, our sub is fucking hot as hell," Adam said. "Those are the most beautiful breasts I've ever seen."

Bane nodded, walking over to the window. "Time for the world to see what is ours, don't you think, bro?"

Her breath caught in her chest.

"Yes, I do. Open the blinds."

Bane smiled wickedly and did.

She felt her heart ramp up in her chest when she saw there were people walking past. At the moment, none seemed to take notice.

Adam stepped behind her, turning her to face the window. "Let's get our sub an audience."

Bane nodded.

Her nerves went into overdrive as Bane began tapping on the glass. *Tap. Tap. Tap.*

Like magic, several of the club's members appeared on the other side of the glass. Sensing their approval, she relaxed some, though her shivers continued running up and down her spine.

Oh my God. I enjoy this. I enjoy being looked at. Bane and Adam saw her as beautiful, and apparently their audience did, too, by the looks on their faces, both men and women. She was so excited and turned on by all the exposure.

"I'm going to remove this thong, sweetheart, and give your audience a complete look at your beautiful body," Adam whispered from behind her. He shoved the lacy thing down to her feet.

She kept her eyes on Bane, but still saw the members break out in applause from the corner of her eye.

"Tell me what's going through that pretty head of yours, sub," Adam commanded. "How does it feel to be on display?"

"It feels intoxicating, Master."

"I bet it does." Adam ran his hands down her sides. "We're going to start by placing you in the sling, sub."

Bane came over, leaving the blinds open. There were more people joining those that had already been watching.

Her two Doms lifted her up and placed her on the sling. They snapped cuffs on her wrists and ankles and then attached the restraints to the sling's chains, which forced her arms and legs up and out, spreading her entire body wide.

"We're going to limit two of your senses so you can focus on our touches, sub." Adam placed a blindfold over her eyes and Bane put some noise-cancelling headphones over her ears. The world became instantly silent and dark. She couldn't even hear her own breathing, though she could feel her chest rising and lowering from her panting. She could feel her heart thudding in her chest, each beat pulsing through her veins. Even her sense of smell seemed heightened as she inhaled Adam and Bane's scents.

Adam lifted one of the headphones off of her ear. "Don't forget to use your safe word if you need it. We can hear even if you can't."

He lowered it back and the silence returned, though her heartbeat sped up. She wondered what they had in mind for her next.

She felt their fingers run up and down her body, delivering stronger sensations than she'd ever felt before from just being touched.

Were the window's blinds still open? Were people still watching? She tingled from head to toe, imagining that they were. Bane and Adam were making sure she got the full experience, and she loved them even more for it.

She felt them place a cube that was very cold on her pussy and she writhed in her restraints. As it began to melt, she guessed it to be ice. Its water ran down between her thighs and she felt her pussy begin to ache.

Another cube was pressed against one nipple and the other, back and forth. But this cube wasn't cold like the ice between her legs. Quite the opposite. Its warmth shot through her like a line of electricity, and both her buds began to jut out and throb.

She moaned into the sweet, dark silence, unable to remain still in the sling. She felt something slightly ticklish, like a feather, run up and down her sides.

She tasted something sweet on her mouth. She licked her lips and tasted honey.

Having only three senses to pull from made this whole experience even more mind blowing than she'd imagined. It was like her sense of taste, smell, and touch had been elevated to levels that were near impossible.

My God, this is incredible.

She could tell they were pouring warm honey on her chest. Adam and Bane began devouring her breasts, each claiming one as their own. They licked her into a frenzied state of building pressure. Their hands roamed up and down her body as they teethed her nipples. Fingers threaded through her pussy, and a thumb pressed on her clit.

She could feel her moans in her throat.

They removed the blindfold and headphones and the rush of sight and sound crashed into her, sending her want even higher.

"That was amazing, but I need you both inside me, Masters." Still restrained by the cuffs that held her to the sling, she was helpless. They were in control. "Please."

"Eager little sub we have, bro," Adam said with a wicked laugh.

"She sure is." Bane pinched her nipples. "Not yet, baby. You have to earn your reward."

"Anything, Master. I'll do anything. Please. I need you. I need you both"

"That's what we like to hear, sub." Bane held a blue butt plug in front of her. "This is for your pretty ass. Going to get it nice and ready for my cock. Understand?"

"Yes, Sir." She watched him lube up the toy and moved it between her legs.

He rubbed the narrow tip over her anus.

"Feel this, sub?" Bane asked, his words reaching a deep, sexy octave.

She nodded.

"This is going to get you ready for me."

She moaned, dying to have him and Adam inside her body. Her need seemed limitless and yet it continued to expand. She wiggled slightly, hoping to find even a sliver of relief.

Adam laughed. "You're burning up inside, aren't you?"

"Yes, Master. So very hot. Please. I need you now or I'll go mad."

"This might help or it might make it worse." He held up a vibrator and clicked it on. The hum of the toy seemed to charge the air around her.

When Adam pressed the vibrator on her swollen folds, Bane sent the plug into her ass. A mingle of pain and pleasure rocked every inch of her body. She shook violently, causing the chains to clang loudly.

"Oh my God, I can't stand much more, Masters. Please. I beg you."

"You will stand much more, sub." Adam stepped back and removed the vibrator, replacing it with his thick fingers inside her. Then he placed the vibrator directly on her throbbing clit, and the pressure multiplied inside her.

"Oh God. This is...so...very...my..." She writhed with overwhelming need, which was straining every cell in her body to the breaking point.

Adam took off his vest, exposing his muscled chest. "There will be no mercy for you, sub. None. You still haven't earned your reward."

"Please, Sir. Tell me what to do. I must have relief. Please."

He smiled, removing the cuffs from her wrists. "You must suck on my cock."

"Yes, Master. Please. I want to taste you. Please."

Bane removed the restraints around her ankles. "Mine, too, sub. When we move you off this sling, the butt plug is staying in. Tighten your ass around it once your feet hit the floor. I'll remove it when I know you're ready."

"Yes, Master."

"I want to feel you on my dick through your hungry lips."

With all her heart she wanted to please him and Adam, to show them she was worthy of her reward.

They lifted her off the sling, placing her on her feet in front of them. The toy in her ass reminded her that Bane had promised to replace it with his thick, long cock once she earned her reward. She couldn't wait.

He removed his vest, tossing it to the side. "Get on your knees."

She obeyed instantly.

"God, you are the perfect sub, sweetheart." Bane's praise sent her to the moon and back. "Take off our pants. Show us how badly you want to have us inside your mouth."

She quickly unbuttoned their pants and slid them off. She wrapped her hands around their hard, monstrous cocks that were so thick she couldn't bring the tips of her fingers to her thumbs. She licked the slits of the heads of their dicks, one at a time. She relished the taste of the salty pearly drops from them.

Adam's hand came down on her shoulder. "Swallow me, sub. Now."

"Yes, Sir." She opened her mouth wide and took in as much of his shaft as she could take, making sure to relax the back of her throat. She bobbed up and down his dick, while pumping Bane's cock with her hand.

She felt a tug on her hair and looked up into Bane's lusty eyes.

"Now me, sub. Do it."

She released Adam and moved to Bane, taking his cock down her throat.

Back and forth between them, she sucked and pumped on their dicks until she could hear their hot, heavy breathing. She squeezed their balls, loving the impact her mouth was having on her two Doms.

They groaned in unison.

Bane pulled on her hair. "Enough. You've earned your reward, sub."

She removed her mouth and hands from his and Adam's cocks and balls.

"On your feet," Adam commanded. "And face me."

"Yes, Sir." Her legs were tingly as she looked up into his face.

He cupped her chin. "You are the most amazing and beautiful woman I've ever laid eyes on, Em."

He called me "Em" instead of "sub." She felt a tingle of warmth spread through her body.

Adam lifted her up into his arms. She wrapped her hands around his neck and her legs around his waist. He thrust his cock into her pussy, causing her to gasp.

Bane removed the plug from her backside and shoved his dick into her ass.

"Oh, God. Yes. Yes. Feels so good, Masters."

"Yes, it does. You feel fucking incredible." Adam's hands were on the back of her thighs as she writhed up and down his cock.

Bane held her from behind. His thrusts were in complete sync with Adam, as they went in and out of her. In and out. Again and again.

They were claiming her for all time. Being between them, having their cocks deep inside her pussy and ass, enjoying every touch from her two Doms sent her into a dizzy state of utter euphoria.

"You like our dicks inside you, sub?" Bane's wicked words worked her up even more.

"Yes, Master."

"God, I love feeling your pussy around my cock." Adam shoved his cock even deeper inside her body.

"Yes. Yes. Yes."

"Come for us, baby." Bane growled. "Come now."

She yelled, unable to hold back the intense orgasm he and Adam had given her.

Squeezing down hard on her two Doms' cocks with her pussy and ass, she felt them both stiffen as they came inside her.

She glanced over at the window and saw the crowd erupt into cheers and applause. She waved at them enthusiastically. Why not? These two men had given her everything. They loved her and she loved them. *With all my heart.*

Chapter Eighteen

Bane handed Emma's granddad a beer.

"Thanks, son. This is quite the party your boss and her husbands are throwing, Em."

"It sure is. I can't wait for everyone to hear the news."

"What news, baby?" Adam asked.

She giggled. "You'll hear in just a minute." She leaned into him. "Just try to be patient."

Emma's grandmother walked up to them with Autumn and Andrea, whose plates were full. "I hope you didn't fill up on the barbeque, Leland."

The dear man patted his stomach. "I only went back three times, Helen."

She shook her head. "If there are any of my pies left, we will have to bring them home and you will have to eat them."

"You brought five pies to this thing, honey." Leland put his arm around her. "I just went to the dessert table. They were a hit. There are only a couple of slices left."

Helen smiled. "I'm so glad. I wasn't sure they were fit to eat."

"Grandma, you know better than that." Andrea laughed. "You make the best pies in the world."

"That's the truth," Autumn chimed in. The sweet young girl turned to him and Adam. "Isn't that right?"

They both nodded. God, he and Adam had fallen for those girls. They'd already talked to Em about adopting them and giving them their name. She'd agreed, saying it would have to be after the wedding, which was planned for mid-September.

Wyatt clinked a butter knife to his glass. "May I have your attention please?"

The crowd settled down.

Mac stood between him and Wade. They were an example of what family meant here in Wilde. It was clear by the looks on the trio's faces that they were madly in love.

"We are so glad that our friends and family are here today." Wyatt put his arm around his lovely wife. "We have some news we want to share with all of you."

"Damn right, we do," Wade chimed in.

Mac smiled. "Guys, don't go off script, please. On three."

In unison they said, "One. Two. Three. We're having a baby."

The crowd roared their joy, cheering like mad.

Bane glanced over at Charly and Shelby, who were showing off their new babies to everyone. Jessie Wilde's little girl, Baby Carol, had just started walking and was entertaining those around her.

Family. That's what it's all about.

Bane looked at the woman he would spend the rest of his life with.

Everything he and Adam had gone through, all the battles around the world, all the pain they had suffered, all of it had led to Emma. She'd come into their lives and changed them. Now they had a new family that included her and her girls and grandparents. He hadn't ever imagined he could be so happy.

He and Adam would always be Marines, but the scars of war faded away just holding Emma in their arms.

THE END

WWW.CHLOELANG.COM

ABOUT THE AUTHOR

Chloe Lang began devouring romance novels during summers between college semesters as a respite to the rigors of her studies. Soon, her lifelong addiction was born, and to this day, she typically reads three or four books every week.

For years, the very shy Chloe tried her hand at writing romance stories, but shared them with no one. After many months of prodding by an author friend, Sophie Oak, she finally relented and let Sophie read one. As the prodding turned to gentle shoves, Chloe ultimately did submit something to Siren-BookStrand. The thrill of a life happened for her when she got the word that her book would be published.

For all titles by Chloe Lang, please visit
www.bookstrand.com/chloe-lang

Siren Publishing, Inc.
www.SirenPublishing.com

CPSIA information can be obtained at www.ICGtesting.com
Printed in the USA
BVOW09s1740151214

379491BV00027B/380/P